Driven by revenge, redeemed by love

When Sigurd, King of Maerr on Norway's west coast, was assassinated and his lands stolen, his five sons, Alarr, Rurik, Sandulf, Danr and Brandt, were forced to flee for their lives.

The brothers swore to avenge their father's death, and now the time has come to fulfill their oath. They will endure battles, uncover secrets and find unexpected love in their quest to reclaim their lands and restore their family's honor!

Join the brothers on their quest in

Stolen by the Viking by Michelle Willingham
Falling for Her Viking Captive by Harper St. George
Conveniently Wed to the Viking by Michelle Styles
Redeeming Her Viking Warrior by Jenni Fletcher
and
Tempted by Her Viking Enemy by Terri Brisbin

Katla was far more dangerous than anyone here believed.

They saw the healer, the caregiver, the dutiful daughter serving her father.

He saw the fierce fighter, the beautiful angel of mercy and the warrior goddess who would protect those she loved. He saw the woman who wanted to throw off her past and embrace a new life.

Worse, he saw a woman he could share a life with. A woman he would be pleased to have at his side, in good and in bad.

All the time he'd thought that the danger to him was from Thorfinn or his men. He'd never considered that a woman would be the weakest part of his plan...or the most powerful.

TERRI
BRISBIN

———

Tempted by Her
Viking Enemy

HARLEQUIN
HISTORICAL

H HARLEQUIN®

® HISTORICAL™

Recycling programs
for this product may
not exist in your area.

ISBN-13: 978-1-335-50581-1

Tempted by Her Viking Enemy

Harlequin Enterprises ULC
22 Adelaide St. West, 40th Floor
Toronto, Ontario M5H 4E3, Canada
www.Harlequin.com

Printed in U.S.A.

When *USA TODAY* bestselling author **Terri Brisbin** is not being a glamorous romance author or in a deadline-writing-binge-o-mania, she's a wife, mom, grandmom and dental hygienist in the southern New Jersey area. A three-time RWA RITA® Award finalist, Terri has had more than forty-five historical and paranormal romance novels, novellas and short stories published since 1998. You can visit her website, www.terribrisbin.com, to learn more about her.

I wrote this book during some of my darkest days and I want to dedicate it to (and thank) all of those readers and authors and friends and family who reached out to me to help me through it. So many shared their own experiences and offered help and consolation and were just... there for me when I needed them most.

Thank you.

Prologue

He loved her. It had taken him a while to be able to acknowledge that truth to himself and then to her, but he knew it now. He loved her.

Brandt Sigurdsson rolled on to his side in the dark of the night and watched his wife sleep. The flames that yet burned in the pit outlined the soft curves of her face as he stared at her. He eased the furs down and watched the way her breasts rose and fell with each breath she took. The sight of his gift, nestled in the valley of her breasts, made him smile.

It marked Ingrid as his. She wore it next to her heart, she said, always to have his touch on her skin.

Smiling at such a thought, he slowly reached out and slid his hand under the furs until it rested on the slight bump there. She shifted and he waited, not wanting to disturb her rest, yet not wanting to remove his hand. Ingrid moved closer to him and rested her head on his arm.

His son.

His son lay within her, growing stronger and bigger each day until he would be born to them.

Brandt spread his fingers across her belly and waited for a sign of something.

Of life.

Ingrid had told him of the quickening only this morn on his return to Maerr after travelling on his father's business for some weeks. A fluttering, she'd called it. As the wings of a butterfly moving on her skin, she'd said. So, in the dark, holding her body to his, he waited, all the while not truly knowing what to expect.

'Did you feel that?' Ingrid spoke quietly and without moving.

Had he awakened her?

'Here. Put your hand here.' She guided his hand so that his fingers rested just above the curls and his palm spread out across her lower belly.

'Now we must pray to the gods to let you feel your son's life in your hand.'

Brandt did as she said and offered up a litany of prayers to any god who would listen. The last one was to Thor, the god to whom he felt an affinity and whose symbol he and Ingrid wore. As he let his mind wait in the silence, something happened. Then, beneath his hand, the tiniest of movements. Not truly movement, but something he could feel shifting within her.

'My son!' he whispered.

'Your son, Brandt.'

She kept her hand over his and held it, pressing on her belly as they waited for another sign.

Awed by the power of such a thing, he held her in

silence. His son. Their son. The babe they had never thought she could carry. That long-awaited child moved within her.

When the moments grew too many and nothing else happened under his hand, Brandt eased a few scant inches away and brought Ingrid on to her back. He moved his hand up to her breasts, where he took the pendant in his hold. He kissed it before tucking it between her breasts and moving over her to kiss her mouth.

'I pray to the gods every day, Ingrid. That you will be brought safely through this. That our son will be born strong and bright. That many, many more will follow.'

He kissed her again, pleased by the way she opened to his tongue, and he tasted and claimed her as his. When she pressed against him and her legs grew restless next to his, he eased his hand back down to the curls between her legs. At her moan, he slid his fingers into the heated place and caressed her slick folds. She let her legs fall open and he moved over her and entered the place, her woman's core, that only he had claimed.

'Ingrid, my love,' he groaned as he pressed the length of his flesh into her. 'I pray...'

No more words were spoken as he worshipped her ripening body and brought her to pleasure. His half of the split pendant he'd had created for them hung from his neck and rested against hers as they found satisfaction.

Concerned that his weight might be uncomfortable

on her, Brandt moved off her, bringing her body to his, not truly wishing to release her yet.

'What else do you pray for, Husband?' she whispered once they'd settled.

'I pray for enough days and nights to show you my love, Wife.' He kissed her. 'For I intend to pleasure you this night.' Another kiss. 'And tomorrow.' He claimed her mouth once more. 'And the next one...' He kissed her until she was breathless once more.

She laughed then, a soft sound that echoed through his body, heart and soul, bringing him pleasure and a sense of ease he'd never expected to feel for her, with her. Their marriage alliance had brought much to his father's kingdom—silver, slaves, furs, land—and he'd expected nothing more. Instead he'd got...her.

'Surely the gods will grant us all the tomorrows we need, Brandt.'

A chill pierced him then, a moment of utter panic, but her nearness eased the feeling.

She continued, 'Aye, Husband, I will pray for all the days and nights so you can show me your love.'

She climbed up over him, straddling his hips with her knees and pressing herself against his flesh. Her full breasts with their darker nipples, made his hands itch to caress them.

'And so I can show you mine, Husband.'

Ingrid leaned down and tasted him, his mouth, his body and his soon rampant flesh.

It was a while before sleep claimed him. They'd joined several more times in that long and special night.

As he lay stroking her hair, she whispered once more. 'All the tomorrows, Brandt. All the tomorrows.'

'All the tomorrows.'

He woke with her words on his lips. Brandt reached out to Ingrid, but his hands met only hard, cold ground now. Climbing to his feet, he looked around and got his bearings. The hide he'd used to fashion a shelter had kept most of the freezing rain and snow off him through the night. The furs at his feet had kept him warm and mostly dry, even though the winter winds tore around him, pulling away any leftover warmth. The bitterness of the cold just pushed the memories away more quickly as he forced himself to move.

Gods, for a moment he'd believed her alive once more and in his arms, giving herself over to the pleasure they'd shared. He pushed his hair out of his face and picked up the furs, rolling them up to keep them dry. Brandt could hear her voice, taste the saltiness of her skin as he licked her body and feel the way she shuddered against him when she cried out in satisfaction. His own flesh rose at those memories.

Cursing loudly, he moved to pack up his camp as he tried to force her out of his thoughts. At least this dream had been better than the usual memories that filled his sleep. The dreams—nay memories that haunted his nights were the sights and sounds of his kith and kin dying before him as he returned to Maerr on his brother's wedding day.

Instead of fighting their enemies at their side when betrayal raised its ugly and deathly head, Brandt had been miles north with his half-brother Rurik when the word reached them. They had rushed back only to find their village aflame, their father murdered along with so many others. Brandt had lost his reason and his control when he saw Ingrid's body with those who'd died.

Ingrid and their soon-to-be-born son.

All he remembered after falling to his knees at her side was the scream that began deep within and would not stop. The temper that was always close to the surface, the one that made him so much like his father, erupted then. When he came back to himself, he found his hands wrapped around his youngest brother's throat, blaming him for not protecting Ingrid as he'd promised Brandt he would and trying to kill him.

Those were the memories he faced in the dark of the night and in the lonely silent times since that terrible day more than three years ago. Those were the memories that had hardened his heart since the treachery that destroyed his family and his life.

He reached up to touch both parts of the pendant he now wore—his and Ingrid's that Sandulf had found by accident when seeking proof that would damn the one behind the plan to kill their father Sigurd and his sons. And, to take their lands, title, wealth and power. That proof—pendants paid to his aunt to keep her sister's secrets that also linked their aunt's husband to the plot—lay carefully hidden inside his tunic waiting to be used.

Searching in one of his bags, Brandt found the dried meat and he took a few minutes to eat it before setting off on the road.

He'd left Danr on Skíð in the west on one of Knut's ships and had then had to cross the entire lands of Sutherland to reach Katanes and his quarry. During the warm months, a voyage on the sea would have been much faster, but in the deep of winter, a trek over land was the only way. The seas were worse and even more treacherous in winter and many boats and men were lost to their anger, much like the anger of the gods that wreaked destruction on the lives of men.

Another three weeks at most and Brandt would finally face the man who'd done his worst to destroy Sigurd and his sons. No matter what happened, no matter if he lived or died, Brandt would restore the honour of his father and bring justice to the innocents whose blood yet called to him.

That need had kept him alive and moving these last years. Through separation and exile, through hardship and kinship, the need for blood to answer for blood drove him. He smiled then, even in the face of the bitter winter wind, and gathered his supplies. As he forced his steps into the snow, Brandt knew the truth. He was close, so close to attaining justice that his blood rose, hungry for the coming fight.

No matter what. He would avenge his father's honour.

He would bring the perpetrator to justice.

He would avenge the death of his wife and their unborn son.

For the thing that had forced him into that brief, overwhelming madness had been the whispered words of someone nearby that acknowledged their baby had indeed been a son.

For the time being, he would control the madness and confront the one responsible. Then he would free the berserker within him and destroy the ones who'd set out to destroy all of them.

Mayhap then he could go back to dreaming of loving Ingrid instead of remembering her death?

Chapter One

Wik Castle, Katanes—Caithness, Scotland
—mid-December in the year of Our Lord 877

The sun's light barely pierced through the thickening clouds this day. So close to the solstice, daylight was a precious commodity here and Katla Thorfinnsdottir was sad to lose more of it to the approaching storm. Wrapping her fur cloak more tightly around her shoulders, she stared into the sky. Aye, a storm grew above, coming from the west and moving towards the sea. From the crisp air and the smell of moisture it carried, this would bring the first heavy snow to Katanes and her father's lands here in Alba.

Finished with the tasks that brought her outside, Katla crossed the yard from the keep to climb the steps leading up to the wall. Their holding was a mix of stone and wooden buildings and structures that mirrored their household. Her mother's Pict blood mixed with her father's Norse. Cousins and workmen and warriors who could claim Gaelic or Pictish or Norse or even ancestors from Eireann—they all made their home here in Wik Castle.

Hardly something as grand as a castle, the stone walls and keep sat on the precipice of land facing the Northern Sea, always braving the strong winds and currents thrown at it from the relentless waters. Katla reached the landing that fronted on the land side of the holding and looked out over the wall towards the village and forest to the south. The winds grew even stronger against her as she stood in silence, but they blew from the land to the sea instead of coming off the churning waters.

Aye, the storm would be a terrible one. Katla turned and spoke again to Enfreth, her late mother's cousin who served as their steward, and trailed her steps.

'The cattle have been brought from the fields? The stores are ready for winter?'

'Aye, lady. We were lucky that it has held off longer this season than most,' he said.

Enfreth was efficient and very experienced, having lived his entire life of three score years here in Katanes. He jested that his bones told him of the change of seasons and the coming of storms and Katla had no reason to challenge his knowledge. Many were skilled at reading the signs of change, whether it be the colours of leaves, the flight of birds or the habits of the creatures of land and sea. She, they, were lucky that Enfreth served Thorfinn Bjornsson and oversaw his holdings here.

Nodding, Katla readied herself to return inside when

the guards in the tower began calling out. She looked in the direction they pointed and saw a man approaching from the south. He was huge, wrapped in furs and alone. One man should not cause such an uproar, so she watched as he walked closer. Unease spread and soon silence reigned as he stood before the gates.

Katla thought him taller even than Arni Gardarsson, her stepmother's commander, and he was the largest man she'd ever seen. This man's head was bare, his long dark hair tied behind his head, and he carried a huge axe in his left hand. His right hand lay on the hilt of a sword that had to be half his height. Spreading his legs and looking like a warrior ready to attack, he leaned his head back and roared out, 'Thorfinn!'

The sound of her father's name shouted with such hatred echoed over the walls and sent slivers of fear through her. She clutched her cloak and froze, unable to move closer to the edge of the wall or farther away. 'Thorfinn Bjornsson, I challenge you!' he called out.

The silence broke then, for the guards were worse than the old women who gossiped in the hall as they wove their wool yarns into cloth. Only Alfaran's arrival stopped them.

'Lady, you should seek the hall,' her father's commander said, as he walked past her. 'I will see to this.'

'Who is he?'

Alfaran reached the edge of the wall and looked over. A moment later, he shook his head and cursed under his breath. 'Davin, seek out the Jarl and tell him to come.'

'Who is it?' she asked once more, never moving from the place where she yet stood.

'No one I ever thought to see again and especially not here,' he said. 'You should seek the comfort of the hall, lady. This will be no place for you to be when your father arrives.'

'Alfaran?' Her father strode from the keep, his sword and scabbard in place, a cloak thrown over his shoulders. His long paces ate up the ground and soon he stood below them, in front of the closed gates. 'Who is it?'

'Brandt Sigurdsson.'

Katla had never seen such power in the utterance of a simple name as she did then. Her father stopped so suddenly he almost pitched forward into the mud and he stood staring at the wooden gates as though he was trying to see right through them. The guards all stared at Alfaran with expressions of shock and disbelief. No one seemed to even draw a breath.

Brandt Sigurdsson?

She had not heard that name in some time. Not since her stepmother, Kolga, had left for her own lands in the north, before the winter seas could trap her here. Peeking over the wall to look at this giant of a man, Katla searched her memories for what she knew about him. He was the eldest son of Kolga's sister Hilda. An outlaw. Banished from the northlands by the King, who placed Kolga's own son in his place. But when the man tugged off his cloak, revealing that he wore only breeches, boots and his sword, she could not think at all.

Coloured markings covered his chest and back and down his arms. The thick pelt of dark hair on his chest only made the contours of his muscles stand out more. When he shifted his stance, she could see the strength of his legs outlined by the tight trews. He was a weapon, fashioned by the gods.

'Are you certain, Alfaran?' her father asked. His momentary shock wore off as he stood beneath his commander.

'Aye, Jarl, 'tis him.'

'I thought him dead,' her father said in a lower voice. It sounded as though he spoke to himself rather than to those around him. 'Open the gates.'

'Jarl?' Alfaran said.

'Father, is it wise to...?' Her voice was louder than she thought and it carried to her father below.

'Open the gates,' he called out. 'Get inside, Katla.'

The wooden bar was lifted by two guards while two more took their places behind their Jarl. Katla began to move away, trying to be the obedient daughter, but her feet would not do so. She needed to find out why this man, whose very name caused such a reaction, was here and what he wanted with her father. If she remembered correctly, though he was an outlaw in the north, he was kin to her stepmother and, as such, should be welcomed and not shouting challenges at her father.

'I thought you would be too cowardly to face me, Thorfinn the Betrayer.'

Brandt Sigurdsson's loud voice carried the insult to everyone who was in the yard or on the walls. It challenged her father once more as he walked out of the gates and stopped there, but this time only to shed his guards. When she would have called out to him, Alfaran grabbed her by the shoulders.

'Hush now, lady,' he said in a stern voice. 'Do not distract him or it could be his death.'

She watched, held in place by the commander's firm grip, as this Brandt backed away from the gates and began to shift from side to side. As a warrior did when deciding how and when to attack. Katla fought against Alfaran's hold.

'You should be down with your Jarl and not keeping me away!' she whispered.

'Do not tell me my duty, lady. I answer to your father and no one else.'

His hands tightened on her shoulders until she gasped from the pain of it. Pulling free then, she rubbed where his hands had hurt her. Men always had to use their superior strength. Men could never accept a woman's challenge though they relished another warrior's.

'Remain, then, if you refuse to follow your father's orders,' he said. 'Know that you will pay on his return for your disobedience.'

Katla moved to the sheltered place at the corner of the wall and watched below. Shivers raced through her body, from both the fear of her father's punishment for disobedience and the danger that filled the air around them. Before she turned her gaze to her father, she noticed Alfaran giving some signals to the other guards. Arrows nocked, several of them moved slowly into positions across the wall. He nodded once more over the wall and she realised that others were in position across the road.

This man who challenged her father stood no chance. He would be dead before he could land a blow.

Staring down at him, she watched as he slowly moved in a circle around her father, his gaze taking in everyone around him as he learned his surroundings. For one brief moment, their gazes collided and she lost her breath at the rage and hatred in his.

'You should not have come, Brandt,' her father answered as he drew his own sword and held it out before him. 'Outlaws have no standing to challenge any free man.' They danced around each other slowly. 'Throw down your sword and I will let you leave with your life.'

'Did you give my father the same treacherous offer before slaughtering him and our kin? Oh, nay, for you were partaking of the hospitality of his household for my brother's wedding, were you not? He had no weapon because he had laid his down.' He spoke in time with his movements and she could feel the tension rise as everyone watching waited for the first strike. 'Betrayer of oaths. Coward who slaughters the innocent. A worthless nithing who killed my wife and unborn child.' He paused after that grave insult to spit on the ground near her father's feet. 'Come now. At least try to meet your death with honour.'

She gasped aloud at such words, unable to believe her father could be such a man as that. He was strong and could be ruthless, but killing a woman with child? Before she could think any further, Brandt Sigurdsson moved, throwing his huge body behind his sword and swinging it at her father.

They moved like the bringers of death they were— both clearly gifted warriors, well experienced in the weapons of power and war. Her father's advantage in years and strength soon gave way to this younger man's relentless hatred and anger. With sword and axe, he battered her father until he fell in the dirt. Even as her father lifted his sword, she knew it would never protect him from the deathblow waiting to end him.

Alfaran whistled then, high-pitched and slow, drawing everyone's attention. Even the man waiting to kill her father paused and looked up. Then he looked around the edge of the wall and into the trees behind him. He cursed loud and long, but did not swing his sword. Before he could speak again or act, her father called out.

'Do not kill him, Alfaran! I owe him an honour debt for saving my life in battle.'

'Jarl!' Alfaran called out. Katla could see the commander did not like his Jarl's orders. Nor did she. Her palms grew wet and a bead of sweat trickled down her back as she waited to watch her father's death.

'Do not kill him!' her father repeated.

'No!' the man screamed out. 'I will kill you!' He swung the sword once over his head and then aimed its sharp and deadly tip at her father's chest. Katla covered her mouth to keep herself from screaming and distracting any of those involved in this death dance.

When Alfaran whistled again, arrows flew, several of them piercing the man's arm and leg and sending him reeling to the ground. Within moments, before she could breathe, the guards were on him, pummelling him until he was unconscious.

'Do not kill him,' her father repeated once more, making the guards stop their assault. Alfaran appeared at her father's side, holding out his hand to help him up off the ground. Then he gathered the man's weapons and brought them to the Jarl.

'Take him inside.' When Alfaran raised his chin as if ready to argue, her father continued, 'I owe him my life. I will not take his. When the weather breaks, I will take him to Harald for judgement.' Alfaran nodded, but her father reached out and stopped him with a hand on his shoulder. 'He will not die in my custody, Alfaran. See to it.'

Katla fell back against the stone wall and forced air into her body. She shook so strongly that she stumbled and needed to hold on to the wall for support. How had this happened? Could any of his accusations be true? She would have to ask her father for the truth, but his temper would be high at this time, from battle and from her disobedience. She would wait until his servants could see to his injuries and until his anger had cooled.

The guards soon gathered in the yard, dragging the huge man into the keep. Her father was still speaking to Alfaran and they were not in agreement from the way their voices rose. Alfaran's hand had been stayed and he was not happy over it, whether the Jarl had wanted the man alive or not. As they walked to the door of the keep, she pressed back into the shadows, hoping they would not see her.

'Daughter!' her father called out without a look in her direction. 'In my chambers. Now.'

From experience, she knew that delaying her arrival when he demanded her obedience would only make his temper, and the punishment, worse. It had been that way with her husband, too. So, she stood away from the wall, gathered her cloak around her and followed him inside. Katla understood that it was better to get it over than to make it worse by dragging out her compliance.

Delaying always made it worse.

Three days later, when she could move her wrenched shoulder once more, Katla made her way down into the underbelly of the keep to where her father held the prisoner. She'd been unable to carry out her duty to take care of injuries and ills these last days and only this morn was able to see to the man who'd challenged her father.

Carrying her basket of medicaments and supplies and a bucket of water, Katla eased down the stone steps and into the darkness. A single torch burned high in a holder on the wall at the far end of the corridor. That no guard was present worried her. She hastened to the locked door and peered through the opening cut in it.

Nothing. She could see nothing. She could hear nothing, no one, moving within. Leaning up and placing her ear closer, she listened again for some sign that he was inside. Then the sound of slow, rasping breaths echoed across the chamber.

'Lady?' She startled and turned towards the man who approached. If she'd not been watching him just then, she would have missed the pity in his gaze. He noticed the bruise on her face and glanced away before speaking. 'Why are you here?'

'My father ordered me to see to the prisoner's injuries. I pray you, open the door.' After another quick look at her face, the guard nodded and slid the key into the lock. He stepped back and Katla pushed it open. 'Bring the torch. I cannot see a thing.'

She could not help the gasp that escaped her when the guard stepped into the cell behind her. First, the horrible smell reached her and she fought not to lose the contents of her stomach right then. Tugging her sleeve down and using it to cover her nose, she took a step and slid...in something.

'Eir, protect him!' she whispered as the light reached the far corner of the chamber and she saw him. 'Bring the light here.'

They'd left the arrows in him! And thrown him here without seeing to his wounds or his condition. She crept closer and listened to the shallow breaths his body took. Katla slipped again and looked at the floor around him. He lay in a growing pool of his own blood. Reaching out, she touched his face and recoiled at the heat of his skin.

'Tell my father that his prisoner is dying.'

'Lady?'

'Go and tell the Jarl that his prisoner will die within the day, if not sooner.' The man went off, clearly not happy to be the one to tell his lord that his orders had not been obeyed.

Katla picked up the skirt of her gown and moved

closer, placing the bucket at his side and her basket on the only clean spot on the floor near him. The least she could do would be to wipe away some of the dirt and blood from his face and be with him when he passed. She dipped a cloth in the bucket and wrung it out before using it on his face. The moan when she touched him surprised her—she'd thought him too close to death to make even a sound. When he turned his face towards the coolness of the cloth and mumbled, she wondered if he might yet live.

'Ingrid?' he whispered, his voice so hoarse and dry she could barely make out the words he uttered. 'Wait for me, Ingrid. Tell our son I am coming.'

His plea tore her heart open and tears made it difficult to see as she continued to minister to him. She prayed to Eir once more to ease his pain. She prayed to Hel to accept him into her hall. She prayed to any god who would listen as she did what she could to make him comfortable.

'Ingrid!' he yelled as he reached out for something.

Someone. His beloved wife for whom he'd come seeking vengeance.

Katla pulled back at the strength of his call, but after a moment, he collapsed on to the floor and made no sound or movement. Had he died then? She placed her hand on the skin of his chest and waited.

Beneath it, his heart beat. Not strong. Not in a regular pace, but it beat.

Mayhap the gods were not done with Brandt Sigurdsson yet?

When her father came in, she told him what she

needed to keep the man alive and he called out orders. Any questions for her father that she had about the connection between the two men would have to wait. All the while, she prayed that the gods had not given up on the man before her. It took her hours to minister to his wounds and, even then, she had no idea if he would survive.

Katla only knew that, for some reason, she hoped he would.

Chapter Two

Surely Surtr had freed himself from Muspelheim and brought the flames of that realm with him here! Brandt fought to keep them from engulfing him, but he was no match for the fire giant who ruled over that world. Was Ragnarök finally upon this world? He pulled with all his might, but the bonds that held him in place allowed the heat to surround and overpower him.

Burning! He was burning without being destroyed and the unrelenting pain forced the screams out of his parched throat. Flames licked his body, leaving scorched skin in their wake. Over and over, until his body was nothing but a charred mass. Then it began anew and the torment continued until he could scream no more.

Mayhap he was caught up in the Christian god's place of punishment instead? The stories of their hell told of everlasting fire and torment to punish sinners. Should he pray to that god for mercy? Anything to ease the pain that tore his body apart. Instead, the old

and new gods taunted him with flaming blows and un-
imaginable heat that pierced his body, his arm, his leg
until he lost himself to it.

Then, he was thrust from Muspelheim's heat to Jö-
tunheimr's cold and hoarfrost. Brandt shook as the ici-
ness penetrated his flesh and bones and tremors from
the shock of it rocked his body. His muscles seized so
strongly he could not breathe. His teeth clattered, then
his jaws clenched so tightly he thought they would
break. The air that moved around him was filled with
shards of frost and it plagued him as it touched his
burning skin. He waited for one of the frost giants
who lived in this land to strike the final blow and end
it. To end him.

But that blow never came.

For hours or days, he knew not which, he was
dragged screaming from one realm to the other, fire to
ice, frost to heat. He could not survive it much longer.

He would not survive it.

Ingrid spoke to him as he suffered the torments of
the gods. He saw his son and longed to join them. To
erase the pain and the emptiness in his heart. His cau-
terised body was empty and his soul longed for the
ease she would give. He heard her whispered prayers
as the gods played with him. He felt her soft touch on
his face, on his body, as she offered what comfort she
could. But who, what woman, could stand up in the
face of the gods' actions and thwart their plans?

Then, it ended. The torture of the heat and freezing cold ended from one breath to the next. Was he

dead? He could not move. He could not open his eyes. Had he died?

Brandt waited for some sign to tell him. Since he'd not been killed in an honourable battle, but slaughtered at their Jarl's orders by those watching, he stood no chance of the Valkyries taking him to the halls of Valhalla. Where would his spirit go then? Would Freyja accept him in Fólkvangr instead?

The touch of a hand on his cheek startled him then. Another on his forehead and then another on his chest. He could feel those. He struggled then to wake fully, but could not.

'Hush now,' the woman whispered. It wasn't Ingrid after all. 'The fever has broken. Rest.' Brandt tried to move, to answer her, to ask her so many things, but his body was not his own yet. 'Take your rest, Brandt Sigurdsson. I will watch over you.'

He let go then of his efforts to awaken and sank into the oblivion of sleep's arms. His questions would wait. She would wait.

She…

Brandt became aware of himself slowly.

As soon as the fog lifted in his thoughts, the pain raced in, making it hard to breathe or think of anything else. At first, he tried to remain still and clenched his teeth against it, but he could not do that for long. Then, it seemed to separate itself into different parts of him—his head ached while his arm and leg burned and screamed with a stronger, more intense pain. When

he considered all of his body, he could find no place
that did not suffer in some way.

What had happened to him?

He remembered approaching the walls of Thorfinn's
fortress and calling out to challenge him. Like the for-
getfulness of a berserker who could bring little else to
mind once engaged in battle, his memories were empty.

The pain he did not forget and he could not ignore
it any longer. Brandt lifted his hand to find the source
of it on his head and could not move. When he tried
the other, the cold, rough touch of iron held it in place.

'Try not to move too much,' a soft voice said. Opening his eyes, he sought her out. A shadow in the corner of the chamber moved and became the form of a
woman as she neared and stepped into the light thrown
by the torch. From the way she struggled to move, he
thought she must be an old crone. 'The wounds were
deep and have only just lately stopped bleeding.'

He tried to lift his head, but the pain stopped him.
What he could see in the dark chamber began to swirl
and dance before him. His stomach twisted and he
fought against the urge to empty it. Yet, at the same
time, it rumbled with emptiness.

'Who are you?' The hoarseness of his voice and
scratchiness of his throat surprised him. 'What happened?'

'You fought Thorfinn. Do you remember?' Brandt
was not so confused that he missed how she did not
answer his first question.

'Nay, not much of that at all. What name are you

called?' He still could not see her clearly, for she stood within the shadows a few yards from him.

'Do you remember your name?' she asked, avoiding his query again.

'I am Brandt Sigurdsson of Maerr. Eldest of King Sigurd. I came here seeking justice and honour,' he spat out, angry now even while exhausted. He pulled the arm that hurt less and the rattling of chains echoed in the chamber. 'And am met with treachery once more. I should have known he could not meet me in a fight worthy of warriors.' He struggled then to speak. 'He could not even kill me as he should have.'

He heard the sigh she released and waited on her words. And waited for her to come closer so he might see her.

'And I am Katla Thorfinnsdottir of Katanes. Eldest of Jarl Thorfinn and his first wife, the lady Modwenna. And you were a fool to think that you would succeed.' In spite of her harsh tone, her touch was gentle when she moved his arm down and shifted the iron ring around his arm to where it did not bite his skin. 'And a bigger fool to think you would find honour here. But at least your thoughts are not as confused as they were when the fever burned through you.'

Brandt leaned his head back and waited for the chamber to stop spinning. He wanted to study his surroundings and decide his next step, but he had not the strength of a flea it seemed. Even focusing his attention on the effort to move his arm or leg did not make it happen. He was so weak and empty.

'How long?' he asked. The woman moved around

the table or bench on which he lay and finally the light from the flickering torch revealed her to him.

Brandt could not tell if his sight was impaired or not, but she looked like a Valkyrie. The way that she'd tightly bound her hair up in large knots behind her head made it impossible for him to see the colour of it. She wore a sleeveless tunic and gown that had little decoration at all. Ah, he understood. This was her work gown, one like many women wore when tending to their chores or fields or seeing to daily tasks. Brandt studied her face and could not help but notice the shadows under her eyes and the leftover dark splotches on her cheek he knew were bruises not yet healed. First... 'How long?'

'Seven days.' Before he could respond to the shock of her answer, he noticed the weariness in her voice and in the way she held herself.

'Seven?' She nodded then, but moved her gaze from his to the furs that covered him.

'I know you wished to die, Sigurd's son, but my father gave me different orders. And for one who claims he sought a warrior's death, you never stopped fighting to live.'

Her words shocked him. He'd been prepared to die, expected to, when he came here. He'd been resigned to seeing Ingrid and his son in the afterlife. So, why had he not welcomed and embraced death when it had been so near to him?

When she leaned over a bit, he saw the wince she tried to hide. Thorfinn's daughter moved around him and, when she began to step away, he grabbed hold of her arm to keep her close. She gasped aloud, the pain evident on her face as she stopped moving for a scant moment before he released her.

'Your pardon. I did not mean to hurt you,' he said as she edged far enough away that he could not reach her.

He had not intended it and doubted he could have caused her harm. Brandt suspected that she had been ill used by someone who had also caused the bruises on her face. Using his strength against women and those weaker had never held the appeal to him that it had for his father and other men. He sensed her fear even across the few paces that were impossible for him to reach or cross.

'I pray I did not cause your injuries while you cared for mine.' He'd recognised her voice as the one that had cut through the haze of pain and suffering. Had she been here the whole time?

'Nay.'

'Are you leaving?'

'I must go. My father…'

Thorfinn the Betrayer, he thought. He heard her knock on the door and then footsteps approaching down the corridor outside wherever this chamber was.

'What happens next, Katla Thorfinnsdottir?' he asked.

'I know not.'

'Then tell your father that I live and let us find out.'

His words sounded bold even to his ears, considering that he could neither move most of his body nor unchain his arm. The key rattling in the lock startled him. They'd locked her inside with him? No matter that he should not be able to cause her any harm, and indeed he could not, but that they so callously exposed her to danger irritated him for some unknown reason.

But he did know part of the reason, for until three years ago, Brandt Sigurdsson had been a fearsome warrior who was respected even by his enemies. And now? A gravely wounded outlaw not worthy of anyone's respect or fear.

'He is awake,' she said to the one who opened the door then. 'I will speak to my father.' The door slammed shut, leaving him in the cold cell, unable to free himself and unable to move.

She was gone, leaving him mired in pain and self-pity. And exhausted. Their brief exchange had used up any strength he'd had and Brandt found himself being pulled back into sleep's grasp. Thoughts and memories began to swirl around him then and he gave up the fight to stay awake.

Katla made her way up the cold corridor to the stairs leading to her father's hall. The storm had come as she'd expected, leaving them buried in deep snow and chilled by icy winds. Every opening in the walls or doors let in the frigid air so that even the huge fire in the main hearth did little to keep the place warm. Midwinter in Katanes was not for the timid or the unprepared.

Or the ill.

Sigurd's son surprised her every day. He should have died before she found him unattended and feverish. The wounds from the arrows had festered and most who'd suffered such would have died from that alone. After removing them and cauterising the many wounds, he still survived. The fever itself should have killed him. Katla had witnessed many who'd gone mad from the pain and heat and others who'd died. Yet, the man had fought through it all.

Though weak as a newly born kitten, she did not doubt he could and would regain his strength. But for what? Her father's plan to return him to the north to face King Harald's judgement was not a merciful thing. A more terrible torture and death would be waiting for him. Katla shuddered, not from the cold but from the thought of what would happen to him.

Her shoulder, aching from the wrenching it had suffered days before and from the cold, grew sore and tight as she walked towards her father. She would seek out an unguent once she had spoken to him.

He sat at table with some of his men. Enfreth stood before him, answering questions that should be hers to answer, but her father had insisted her duty was to see to the prisoner's injuries. Katla had not slept well in days and had eaten little since rising from her bed four days ago.

'Katla,' her father called out. 'Come.' Enfreth stepped away and Katla came closer, not to a stool but to the place her father indicated with a wave of his hand. 'Tell me of Sigurd's son's condition. Will he live?'

Glancing at the others sitting or standing at her father's side, she noticed a variety of expressions that told her what his men thought about keeping a Norseman alive in their dungeons. To a one, she was met with angry and suspicious glares. But Alfaran's was the one that worried her the most. No matter her father's rebuke of his commander when Brandt was taken prisoner, Alfaran still argued for his death.

'The fever has broken. The wounds seem to be healing. He is too weak for me to declare him well...yet.'

A wave of dizziness swept over her then as she waited on her father's reply. Her legs grew weaker until she thought she might fall. Black spots and flashes of light filled her vision forcing her to reach out for support to stand.

'Katla?' her father called out in a strange voice.

Then the world grew dark.

'She wakes,' the whispering voice announced to someone.

Her servant, Aife, was the whispering one. Katla began to open her eyes, but when the chamber around her swirled and shifted, she stopped trying. The whispering voice blended with other hushed voices that surrounded her for a short time. If her aunt and sister were there, she had no choice but to try again. Clutching the surface beneath her, she held on tightly and opened her eyes. Gemma sat at her side, looking more like a terrified child than the young woman she was becoming.

'Katla!' she cried out. 'What happened to you?'

'Gemma, I am well,' Katla said. With Aife's assistance, she pushed herself up on her elbows even as the dizziness threatened to make a liar of her. Still, no matter the cause, she did not want her sister worrying. 'I am just tired. You can go, Aife.' Thankfully,

Gemma waited for the girl to leave before she continued her questions.

'Father said the Norseman hit you and you collapsed because of him.'

Katla struggled upright and pushed her loosened hair out of her face. She'd always managed to keep the worst of her father's harsh behaviour from her younger sister. She'd covered up bruises and sprains and worse to avoid the questions and, even more dangerous, her sister's unfailing loyalty and habit of trying to step into matters she knew not of. If Gemma tried to intervene, Katla could not imagine the consequences. So far, only she, the elder one, had been the target of their father's harsh anger. Katla had sworn to their mother on her deathbed to protect Gemma. And she would.

'He did not hit me, Gemma,' she explained as she met the knowing gaze of their elderly aunt. 'He did grab my arm and tug on it.' She reached up and felt the shoulder joint that had screamed in pain at his strong pull. ''Tis not quite healed from my fall in the yard.' The thick snow that blanketed the area as she'd predicted had been packed down into ice by the footsteps of all who traversed the yard and she'd used that as her excuse for the most recent injuries.

'Is he terrifying? They said he challenged Father and his men by himself? Armed with only a sword?'

Though not many had witnessed the exchange or the short fight, gossip had spread widely and wildly over what had happened between Sigurd's son and her father. Some of the men serving her father knew of Brandt and knew of his family's downfall in the north-

ern lands ruled by King Harald. Those bits of knowledge, coupled with rumours and tales, spread quickly
among those trapped inside due to the bitter winter
storms that relentlessly passed over them on their path
to the sea.

The other thing she considered before answering
her sister was Gemma's innate curiosity. If Katla made
the prisoner sound interesting or intriguing—more so
than the current gossip had done—Gemma would seek
him out. Sadly, her sister's curiosity and wonder had
not been tempered by fear or sense. So, she chose her
words carefully.

'Right now, the man is half-dead in the cell below.
He is an outlaw and not a man of honour who can challenge our father, Gemma.' Her stomach twisted at those
words. From his explanation, he seemed more honourable than most men, warriors or nobles that she knew.
'Only the gods will decide if he dies or lives to face the
King's justice.' Gemma's expression fell at her words
and Katla thanked the gods for that.

'So, he may yet die?' Katla nodded. 'He was not
terrifying?'

'Not to Father or his men. Father met him sword
to sword.' How much of the truth had she heard? Did
she know that it was only the intervention of Alfaran
that had saved their father's life? That the Norseman
had been a moment away from taking her father's life?

Gemma thought on that for a moment before nodding her head. 'I hope the gods show no mercy to such
a man as he.'

Her aunt's cough drew Katla's attention. The worry

she could see in Alpia's eyes did not foretell good things. Katla shifted to the side of the pallet, moving slowly because the dizziness yet threatened her balance. As she stood, her head and shoulder ached again.

'You lost consciousness and fell to the floor. I tried to check for injuries, but...' her aunt said. 'Are you well enough to leave your pallet yet?'

Realising that Gemma was watching and listening to every word, Katla nodded. 'Gemma, go to the kitchen and ask for some strong broth and bring it here.' Once her sister left their chamber, she turned to her aunt. 'What has happened?' Only then did she notice that the lamps were lit. 'Has night fallen?'

'Aye, and another day and into the next night since you fell ill again.'

Two days had passed? What had caused such a thing?

'You hit your head when your father struck you, did you not? You fell against the wall before he wrenched you back, spraining your shoulder?' her aunt asked.

Katla did not wish to discuss the specifics of her father's most recent blow with her aunt, but she knew the old woman would not cease until she got the details she sought.

'Aye, I hit my head on the wall.'

'Your father struck you. You did nothing.'

They'd had this battle before—she tried to explain away the reasons or the injuries she suffered and her aunt refused to allow her to take the blame. Since her father had never aimed his temper at her aunt, Katla simply went along with her, knowing it was easier that way. 'Aye.'

'A blow that like can knock you senseless immediately or it can continue to make you confused and weakened for a long time after. You returned to your duties too quickly. You should have rested.'

'And I must return to them again.' Her aunt reached out and took her hand to stop her. When she might have resisted and pulled away, her shoulder reminded her of the folly of such a movement. 'Aunt Alpia, Brandt will die without help.'

'Brandt, is it?'

'He was placed in my care—'

'You were ordered to do so.'

'He will die.'

'And you care? About the man who insulted your father's honour and attacked him?'

'Why are you doing this, Aunt?' Katla asked. 'My father has ordered me to see to this man's injuries. My father does not care that I am not well or too weak to do his bidding. I cannot take the chance that his anger will…' She could not voice her true fear openly. To say it would somehow, she worried, make it happen and put her sister in danger. She peeled her aunt's fingers from around her wrist and stepped away slowly, praying that the dizziness would cease. 'I will see to my duties.' Her aunt's gaze seemed to penetrate her soul in that moment.

'He yet lives, Katla. I have been seeing to him these last two days while you were unable.' She faced her aunt. 'He is able to remain awake for an hour or two at most and can drink broth or watered ale.'

'The fever?'

'A slight one.' When Katla turned away, her aunt continued. 'Have a care, Niece.' Katla nodded and turned to leave, but her aunt was not finished yet. When the older woman lifted her hand to touch Katla's cheek, she could not stop the need to flinch at the contact. 'I know your life is a hard one, made harder by your father's anger. And it is not the one of your choosing, Katla. I know that your marriage was not—'

'Do not speak of that!' Katla said. She did not wish to think on those months when she'd barely survived.

'But, Katla, truly you must have a care with this matter. He is your father's enemy and nothing good can come from this.'

Tears burned in her throat and Katla could not reply to the caring concern in her aunt's voice and words in spite of her anger over Alpia's choice of words. She nodded and then strode from the chamber in haste, searching for Gemma and the broth, avoiding the hall and any of the places her father might be.

Winter, with its long nights, played hard on their dispositions here when the snowstorms and brutal cold forced them indoors for lengthy stays. Tempers flared. Fights ensued. Her father's strong rule kept things from being deadly, but one could never predict when he would lose his temper and, then, no one was truly safe.

She crept through the corridors to the stairway leading below. Shivering against the cold, she tugged her shawl around her. The thick stone walls were no match for the winter winds down here and the torches flickered from the chilling air as it moved through this dank corridor. Katla held her breath as she approached the cell where Brandt was held, not truly knowing what she would find this time.

Chapter Three

The swirling chilled air drawn through the cracks in the stones told him someone approached. Each time the door somewhere down the corridor opened, the cold swirled in. The bitter winds of their lands had never bothered him before, but he'd never faced them in this condition. He felt weaker than a baby left outside to face the judgement of the gods.

The old woman who had come in Thorfinn's daughter's stead had at least left a thick fur over him to keep away the worst of it. And she'd seen to his needs with a quick efficiency that spoke of the experience of a healer. When he'd asked about Katla, she would say nothing.

Over the last two days, Brandt had begun to recover. He woke and slept more regularly. He could hold his own head up when offered a cup or bowl. The pain was his constant companion, but he refused when the old woman offered him something for it. He needed his wits about him if he was going to figure out a way out of this. Or a way to confront Thorfinn again. Or another path, for this one was not one he could accept.

Face King Harald's 'justice'? There was none to face. Already, the same King who had forced hundreds, nay, thousands of his countrymen out to find new lands and places to conquer had accepted the words of liars and murderers and chosen to back them rather than the sons of Sigurd who were the rightful heirs to their father. They'd spent the last few years searching for the truth behind their father's murder and those who had plotted it, and he would not stop in claiming vengeance for all those who died.

So, remaining here as Thorfinn's prisoner was not something he could or would accept. But, when he tried to pull himself up to see who approached, Brandt knew he had many challenges ahead before he could finally grasp the satisfaction he needed.

He managed to turn and lift his head without jostling his injured arm and leg to look as the door opened. It was…her. And once again she moved more like the old woman who'd treated him than the young one she was. Pain was evident in each movement that involved her arm as he watched her get closer. The lamp left by the old woman exposed the weakness to him and he continued to observe her as she walked to his side.

A blush filled her cheeks as she met his eyes, before she quickly averted hers. He was more interested in the bruises beneath her eyes as he studied her. She favoured her one arm as she tugged her shawl closer around her. A wince gave it away. It was the same one he'd tugged on two days ago. Brandt knew what he would find if he drew off her gown and looked—a wealth of old bruises and welts in a differing pattern of healing.

She'd been injured or beaten over time. He would swear he had seen the outline of a man's hand on the side of her face. Had Thorfinn struck her so? Or…a husband? He shook himself then. How she'd come to be injured was none of his concern. A man had the right to discipline or punish those in his control for disobedience and other sins as he chose. Though something tickled at his thoughts then, for he'd never known Thorfinn to be so much like his own father, Sigurd, in this regard.

But the man he'd known would never have committed such a treasonous action against his own friends and allies. Brandt wondered if he'd ever truly known this man. The important thing was that how Thorfinn treated his own daughter mattered little or not at all to Brandt. It should not matter.

'How do you fare?' she asked, breaking into his reverie.

'I am alive.'

'That is more than I expected since your arrival here,' she said. 'Do you feel strong enough to sit up?'

'Why?'

'You are able to drink?' At his nod, she said, 'I brought you some broth.' He watched her as she placed the bowl on the table and turned back to him. He had not moved yet.

'Do you intend to linger until you die or do you wish to live?' Her voice was sharp and tinged with impatience. 'You are lucky to be among the living. Mayhap the gods decided to show you mercy? Should you spit in the face of that with your lack of effort after they have gifted you so?'

Damn, but her words made him more curious than he wished to be! Anger. Impatience. Bitterness. All that and more flowed like a current under the words she spoke.

'I would think that Thorfinn's daughter would wish me dead, just as her father does.' He'd said it as a way to decipher her anger and bitterness. Against his own wishes, she'd intrigued him.

'At first, I did. But now I do not want all my efforts to be for naught.'

He laughed at her words. Well, he wanted to laugh, but his body fought him and the laugh turned into a spasm of coughing that left him weak once more. When he could draw breath, he whispered, 'Ah, but your father and the King will surely undo all your work in due time.'

Something sparked in her green eyes. If he'd not been watching her closely just then, he'd have missed it. It lasted only moments before disappearing, leaving him wondering over its cause. She dropped her shawl and stepped to him.

''Tis at my father's command that I do this. Come,' she said as she slid her hand and then her forearm beneath his neck where it met his shoulders. She still wore the sleeveless gown and so her skin touched his. 'Try to sit up. Slowly, slowly.'

For no other reason but to do as she asked, Brandt

began to lift his head at her guidance. She moved closer now, her arm behind his shoulders and her head near his. Close enough for the bruising on her cheek to be seen clearly. His attention on her, the touch of her skin on his, the softness of her breasts as she leaned in to guide him, made him unaware of the terrible sensation in his stomach until it was too late.

Without delay, she aided him as the dizziness and nausea hit him. His head swam and his gut rebelled this attempt to remain upright and he could not. Even in his damnable distress, she was there, holding his head and then guiding him back down. More surprising was the gentleness in her touch in caring for him even though she spoke of commands or orders to do so.

Neither one spoke for a while as he settled back, praying all the while that he would not be humiliated in such a manner again. No matter what had happened when he was senseless, being aware of the need to be treated like a helpless babe was not something he could bear easily.

And yet, mayhap he would yield to her gentle ministrations and leave the fight for later.

When she left the cell soon after that, he turned his face to the wall and listened to the sound of her steps that took her away. Later, as the cold winds invaded, he thought about that expression in her eyes. The one he could not explain or describe. She'd brought something to mind in that moment. Something that had startled her and she'd given that away to him without realising it.

Exhaustion overwhelmed him then—the struggle

to sit and its consequences had taken all his strength. He would think about her reaction and what it meant... later.

The following days flowed one into the next, pain filling his waking hours and nightmares his sleeping. Then, only when things changed, Brandt realised he was getting stronger and recovering a bit more with each passing day. It took another week before his head felt clear enough to sit for an extended time and for his stomach to agree. His wounds stopped bleeding or seeping and soon closed. He could stand up and move as far as the chain allowed.

He was not comfortable, but he was not neglected as many prisoners would be. Garments had been provided for him and his own shoes and cloak returned. Food came at regular intervals—plain and filling and much like his family ate during the long nights of winter. His chest tightened as the memories of those nights flowed freely in his thoughts.

His brothers, his mother, his friends... Ingrid. Nights passed drinking ale around the fire in the longhouse or playing games with his brothers, especially Alarr who loved to win at *tafl*. The game required much practice to control the pieces and to win and Brandt was proud of Alarr's effort to learn and succeed. Though, to be honest, Brandt's pride was tempered by his own need to win.

The other memories that flooded in in the empty hours were those of the time spent in the furs with Ingrid while the winter winds howled outside. Thank the gods for those long nights of pleasure…and love. Those seemed more real to him since that strange dream he'd had on his journey here.

By his estimate of the days that had passed and from things he noticed happening here in the keep, it had to be early into the new year. He'd heard complaints from the guards for weeks now about the unceasing snow and strong storms and from Katla herself when she did speak to him of matters other than his condition.

Katla arrived at some point each day, though the time varied depending on her other duties. From what he knew or had gleaned from bits of conversation overheard, she oversaw running her father's estate here in Katanes. The household was her domain while the steward controlled the fields and farms and their commander Alfaran, who was Thorfinn's cousin from near Maerr, oversaw the warriors who were a mix of Norsemen from Thorfinn's lands in the north and local men raised and trained here, from the household of his first wife's family.

She stepped widely around him once he sat up or stood and he could see the fear in her eyes as she did so. Though her bruises had faded as his wounds healed, she yet startled with any quick move he made. Finally, one day, the relentless terror in her gaze was the thing that let his temper loose. A temper he'd not felt in many, many weeks.

Even knowing it would make things worse, he could not stop himself from standing when she entered the cell. He waited for her to meet his eyes.

'Have I harmed you, Thorfinn's daughter?' He took another shortened step, taking him to the full length of his chain. 'Have I raised my hand to you as others clearly have?' Her gasp echoed between them and those eyes the colour of the moss in summer stared into his. 'Have I?' he demanded. When she did not or could not reply, he lifted his chin and narrowed his gaze. 'So, was it your father who struck you or do you have a husband who raises his fist to you?'

She tripped backwards in surprise and would have fallen against the wall if he'd not grabbed for her and taken hold of the cloak she wore. When she regained her balance, he released her cloak with haste and stepped back a few paces.

'Every time you enter this cell, you look on me with terror in your eyes. You move around me as though I am stalking you.' He lifted his hand quickly and watched her react as he suspected she would. 'You but wait for me to strike as though others have told you I would. Have they, Katla? Have they warned you that I am a caged beast simply waiting to tear you apart?'

Strangely, for the first time since he had faced Thorfinn, he felt alive and aware. His chest heaved with anger. He was weaker still, aye. Yet, as he tightened his hands into fists and then relaxed them once more, he noticed that the pain was gone. He turned his attention back to the woman before him—the one responsible for giving him his life back. The one who'd stirred this reaction in him.

She stared, wide-eyed, and watched his every move, her green gaze flicking back and forth from him to the door of the cell. Like a wounded animal seeking an escape. His words had done that to her. More than that, he was certain that others had instilled this fear in her.

They had warned her.

Chapter Four

They had warned her.

Indeed, of exactly such a thing as this.

Stories were told in the hall above of this man's temper and the damage he did while under its influence. Just like his father, they whispered. Dangerous. Deadly. Just like her husband had been.

Brandt, it seemed, would survive his wounds and so her father urged her to turn his care over to another. He'd not commanded her to do that yet, so she would continue. Yet she'd seen no sign of the prisoner's rumoured temper or dangerous behaviour turned towards her. Until only recently, he'd been too sick and too weak to do anything but recover and try to live.

'Aye,' she managed to stutter out. 'I have been told of your strength and your temper. Of the danger in coming close to you since you are out of your sickbed.' Out of it, aye, but even now he began to wobble as he stood there angrily confronting her.

He was angry. It flashed in his icy blue eyes. His

breathing increased and his hands clenched into fists
as he watched her. Fear that she'd disregarded as unim-
portant grew within her. Fear that could even save her
life. All those stories told about him ended with him
losing his temper and people dying. But the part of her
who had worked so long and so hard for his survival
was somehow glad to see this change in him.

For once, her father and stepmother's plans were
thwarted.

Katla could not spend a moment pondering on that
strange thought because Brandt began to tilt and she
knew he was going to fall. She went to his side without hesitation and slid under his uninjured arm to support him.

'Sit down here,' she ordered. 'If you fall, you will
have to lie where you land for I have not the strength
to pick you up.' When he leaned on her and took a few
steps back to the pallet behind him, she wondered if
they both wouldn't fall then.

'You speak of my temper, Katla Thorfinnsdottir,'
he said as he accepted her help. 'I think 'tis you they
live in fear of with the way you bark out your orders.'
He laughed then, even as he dropped the last distance
to the pallet with a groan. 'Aye. I think they tell you
tales of me because they fear you.'

He was jesting with her. He was jesting? This was
the first exchange she remembered that involved something other than questions about his condition or his
care or about the weather outside.

'If that were only true, Brandt Sigurdsson.'

He laughed again as he adjusted his body on the pallet to keep the chains from pulling on his healing arm. 'Women never see the power they hold.'

Her stepmother did. And she used it ruthlessly for her own desires. His laughter dissolved away and he frowned at her.

'I meant no insult to you,' he said. 'I see the signs on you that you have been used roughly and do not like to see that on any woman.' He lifted his arms and ran his hands through his unruly hair. He could move both easily. Another sign of his recovery. 'No matter what you were told, I have never raised a hand to a woman and never will.' He nodded at her. 'Especially not one who saved my life when she could—and should—have let me die.'

How could she reply to his words? He had noticed her fears and the bruises she wore and somehow was angered by them. Those living here ignored most of the marks of her father's anger and only prayed that they would not be on the wrong end of her father's attentions next.

As she stared at this stranger, it struck her that her father had not always been this way towards her. He seemed to live in constant anger at her, as though he'd found her wanting in some way these last few years. Before that, he had been a good father to her and Gemma, even after their mother died. Somewhat distant and sometimes harsh in his reprimands, he expected to be obeyed and obeyed quickly. Punishment came quickly after disobedience, yet never had he been as brutal as over these last four or so years.

After her mother's death, her father had been interested in her abilities and had encouraged her to take on responsibilities in his household. He'd acknowledged her place and her duties with respect.

Then, nigh on five years past, everything had changed—*he* had changed. While on his lands in the north, he'd married Kolga, sister by marriage to Sigurd, without telling anyone of his plans. He'd returned here, to their home, with a wife who was then in charge of the household and ultimately Katla and Gemma. One who had her own lands. And a nearly grown son. A wife with plans of her own, it seemed.

In the midst of all those changes, something else had altered as well. Her father refused to carry out her mother's wish that she marry a man descended from the local people, the Picti as they were being called, and married her instead to a man of her stepmother's choosing.

Things had gone wrong ever since.

Brandt coughed and brought her attention back to him.

'I would give you my word, my bond, if you would accept it from me. If it would make you more at ease here.' He motioned around the small cell. 'I swear that I will not harm you.'

For some reason, she believed his words. She believed them even when she had learned to mistrust promises made by men who wanted something. Or who had power over you. But his words and this promise reassured her. This day seemed to be the day of strange and rebellious thoughts. She nodded.

'I accept.'

'You do?' His eyes lit in surprise then. 'You do.' He nodded back. 'What brings you here this day?'

Katla let out the breath she'd been half-holding in all the way down here. The one she lived holding in as she walked this keep and these lands. Always waiting to learn if this would be the time when her father struck out at her. Always confused over what had turned her father against her. Waiting to learn that her efforts to keep Gemma safe had been for naught.

''Tis time to remove the last of the bandages.' She picked up her basket from where she'd left it and walked to where he sat.

He watched her movements in silence as she unwrapped the lengthy bandages that encircled his arm. Bringing the lamp closer to inspect the area, she slid her fingers over the places where the arrows had pierced his flesh. Two had hit his arm and both had healed.

'Your markings do not match now,' she remarked, sliding her fingers over the scars that spread across his skin. 'The swirls do not meet.' Her fingers traced the pattern on his arm as she spoke.

His skin was smooth and the markings were remarkable in their design. Swirls, pictures made of symbols of the gods, animals and creatures from stories covered his chest and stomach and arms. It must have taken months of painstaking work to create such intricate forms. Only when she realised that his breathing had stilled did she look up and meet his intense gaze.

One moment turned into two and then three as she noticed the flare in his eyes that spoke of one thing.

She dropped his arm and busied herself searching her basket for some needed item.

'No matter,' he said. 'Once the healing is complete, the scarring will fade into the design.' She'd never seen a man so covered in markings before.

'Will it? Will they?' Katla nodded at the other places that had been injured.

'Aye. It has happened before. The markings were completed some years ago and I have been injured many times since. You do not see most of them, do you?' He sat up and turned his back to her for her inspection. 'The worst one is the one that runs from the bottom of my ribs up to my shoulder here.' He shrugged his right shoulder.

Without thinking, she lifted her hand and let her fingers trace the length of the scar once she'd found it. He was right—it disappeared into the patterns if you did not know where to look for it. He stilled beneath her touch then.

Katla wanted to trace the rest of the markings and to feel the powerful muscles that gave them contours and movements. After a moment, she resisted that urge—another rebellious thought—and lifted her hand from his warm skin. She breathed in slowly, trying to calm her racing heart, and let it out.

'Did one person do all of these?' she asked. In spite of her unseemly reaction to touching him after all these weeks of never noticing, her curiosity won out over her restraint.

'A holy man who lived in our village. He saw patterns in everything he looked upon and could paint or mark the images on skin.'

'I have never seen so many on a man from the north.' His brow raised in question. 'My ancestors who lived on these lands used such markings, whether placed under the skin as yours are or painted on for battle.'

'You are not Norse?'

'Nay. Well, I am half-Norse. You know that my father is, while my mother descended from the local people.'

Her ancestors had lived and controlled all of the lands here until the assimilation with new visitors and conquerors buried their customs and their history. Like the custom of inheriting through their mothers' bloodlines. Many things had faded into oblivion since the Norsemen moved into this place.

Without thinking, she moved to the next area that needed tending—his leg. It took only a moment to realise the foolhardiness of her actions.

No longer was he a man so weak that he could not rise from his pallet. Nay, he was moving ably and dressed in garments that would need to be removed to examine the healing wounds on his thigh. She could not find her breath at such a thought.

'The wounds look much as these do,' he said in a soft voice. 'No redness or swelling.'

Katla swallowed against the tightness in her throat... twice before she could speak. 'You have checked them?'

'Aye. And so has the old woman.'

'Alpia. My mother's sister.'

'She is not as fair to look upon when she tends my wounds. Or when she forced me to drink those horrible draughts.' He laughed once more and the deep sound of it echoed across the cell.

Katla smiled, trying to find words to say to him. No one here remarked on her appearance. No one dared speak of it, for to do so would force them to acknowledge the times when they could not. The times when the marks of fists or hands had marred her skin. Or worse, when they witnessed her father strike out. No one ever spoke of anything but her abilities and skills. But this man did.

'She taught me much of what I know about healing and herbs. If Alpia said they are healed, I accept her word on it,' she said, neatly avoiding any other parts of what he'd said. Katla stood then and took her basket in hand.

'Will you return?' he asked. He settled on the pallet slowly; the rattling of the chains as he adjusted them was louder than his voice.

'Return?'

'Aye, return here. To this cell. Or are your duties complete?'

'If you have need of me…' she walked to the door before turning back to him '…ask one of the guards to send for me.'

'I would ask a favour of you before you go, Katla.' His deep voice sent shivers deep inside of her.

'I do not know if I have the power to grant you any favours.'

She wanted to leave, yet she waited to hear his request. He'd not asked for anything from her during his weeks in this situation. Oh, he'd begged her to let him die in the first days, yet that had changed after he survived the terrible fever with its delusional visions and imagined visitations from his dead kin…and wife.

So many possibilities flooded her thoughts then, about all the things he could need or want. So many things that would be denied. So many things unnecessary to a man facing execution soon. Katla held her breath until he spoke.

'I would ask for two buckets of water and some soap.' Not what she'd expected or anything she would have guessed if asked to do so. 'Though you have done well at keeping my wounds clean, I wish to wash the rest.'

'I will see if I can arrange that,' she said.

'My thanks.'

His words startled her, for she'd not expected gratitude to be expressed either. Yet, those Norse she knew preferred to be clean, even through the coldest of winters, availing themselves of hot springs in their lands. She called out to the guard and waited for the door to open. Only as she walked up the stairs did the image come unbidden into her thoughts.

Brandt Sigurdsson standing in that cell, washing himself. The contours of his body, the colours of the markings on his skin, his long dark hair, all wet as he scrubbed off the grime of the weeks spent here imprisoned. For a moment, another rebellious thought played within her—her hands were the ones scrubbing him clean. Rubbing the soft soap over his arms and shoulders and down past his waist to his legs and those strong thighs that stretched his trews to almost bursting.

Her body responded to such thoughts and it surprised her. She'd never cared for bed play and the times her husband had taken her had not been something she'd wanted. But this stranger, this outlaw, kindled a heat deep within her loins that both shocked and shamed her. Katla hurried her pace, trying to force every forbidden image from her thoughts as she went.

It was some time before the mundane chores in the keep distracted her enough from those thoughts, but she managed to banish them. Her father had asked for a gathering at the evening meal this day which meant additional work for her to arrange. Truly, it could not have happened at a better moment.

At some time during those next hours, she did ask one of the guards and a servant from the kitchen to deliver the water and soap to the prisoner. When her father arrived at table, he asked that Katla and Gemma sit at his side. A deep and strong unease filled her as she did as he'd asked. When her father's strange mood continued through supper, Katla felt the tightness in her growing moment by moment until she could barely sit quietly at his side. The furtive glances sent in her direction by her aunt and Enfreth caused her stomach to clench.

This could not be a good thing. This would bring bad tidings, of that she had no doubt. The fact that he had asked for both of them worried her more than anything. He'd not singled out Gemma for attention before. Not like this. Finally, he pushed away from the table and stood. Katla grabbed hold of the table's edge to keep herself from screaming at what was to come.

And then he spoke.

Chapter Five

'My daughter… Katla does not think I know her worth,' he said loudly to those gathered. With a nod at her, he continued, 'But I do. We all do!' He lifted his cup and everyone present raised theirs. Her stomach clenched and threatened to release the little she'd consumed. 'To Katla!'

Katla forced a smile on to her face as her father watched her. Those around her nodded and smiled back. She could not take in a breath. Her chest burned with the need for it, but she fought to control every part of herself as he spoke. Her face froze, she drew in a shallow breath and waited for the worst, for it was yet to come.

'These last years she has ruled Wik Castle in my absence and sometimes even when I was here!' He laughed and his men joined in. Alfaran's smile did not quite reach his eyes. He had never been happy when she had sat in her father's place. He'd never been happy with anything that she did. In Enfreth's gaze she recognised worry. 'I am happy to tell you and her...' he paused with a glance at her '...that I have accepted a marriage proposal for her from my wife's commander, Arni Gardarsson!'

She felt nothing. Not the air around her nor the table in her grasp. Empty.

She heard nothing. The rest of his words and the sounds of cheering faded into an unnatural silence.

She saw nothing. The hall and those before her disappeared in a black haze that swirled around her until it contracted so thickly she thought she would die.

Oh, she would die. If the threatening darkness did not take her, Arni Gardarsson would break her apart piece by piece until nothing was left of her. Nothing left alive.

She knew his kind. She'd seen it in his behaviour and heard it in his whispered threats whenever he was here. He'd wanted her, in his bed, and she'd refused him. Oh, as a widow she could have slept with him or any man, but as a woman, she understood what he wanted from her was not bed play. He wanted to tear down the Jarl's daughter for spurning him and to destroy her at his leisure.

Her father had protected her in the past. Whether he'd known the truth about her first husband or not. Whether he'd heard of Arni's plans for her or not, he had forbidden such a match.

Until now.

His voice broke into the silence that extended through the whole of the hall and she realised that he waited on her to speak. And what could she say? The decision had been made. He would never have mentioned it if both he and his wife had not come to some agreement over it. As she pushed her chair back slowly and stood, she saw the profound gaze her father cast at Gemma and understood its meaning. So, she played the part as she must and would find answers later.

'I thank you for the honour of this match, Father.'

The hall exploded into raucous and deafening cheering at her words. From the expressions, some were happy for her, some were happy that the Jarl's words would be obeyed and others would be happy to be rid of her. Only Alpia's, Gemma's and Enfreth's held any affection or true concern.

She suffered through the next hours, accepting the well wishes of those who offered them and watching her father in any moment she could. Something was wrong here. He had no respect for Arni, though he would never say it openly. She'd overheard her father's comments to Alfaran when the man came or left with Kolga and knew he belittled him whenever he could.

So, why would he approve of this marriage?

Finally, the evening ended when her father rose and left the table, without ever speaking to her directly. Katla leaned back in her chair and allowed her body to relax against the hard back even while waving off Aife's approach. Drinking deeply, she thought on her possible actions in this matter. In spite of her words, she could never willingly walk into this marriage. No more than an animal would walk up to its predator and offer its neck.

So, how could she avoid it?

Oh, as a woman in the world of the Norse she had the right to divorce her husband. But first she had to survive long enough to ask for one. And Arni would kill her before he would let her shame him with a divorce. Her thoughts twisted and turned, in fear and frustration, and she could see no path forward.

Until she spoke to her father about this unholy arrangement, she had no idea what to do or where to turn. She suspected that Kolga had instigated this after Arni had pushed Katla to take him to her bed and she'd refused. Though she'd never openly spoken of the incident—incidents, for he'd tried several times—to her father, she did not doubt that he knew of them.

Placing her cup on the table, she stood then and waved the other servants in to finish cleaning the table and clearing the hall for night time. They should not be held up in their chores because she could not decide what to do. From the strange feeling within her—one of shocked numbness rather than the anger she'd expected to bloom at this news—Katla knew that she would feel more later. When it was safe to do so. When no one could see or hear her.

In the dark of the night where all her fears came to life.

Deciding to wait until the next morning to speak to her father, she moved silently through the rest of her evening chores, making certain the cook had what he needed for the morrow's meals and such. When she finished and could go to her bed, a restlessness filled her that she knew would make it impossible to get any sleep. So, she found her cloak and left the hall, climbing the steps to the top of the wall where she could see the sky and the sea on one side, the village and the road on the other.

The crunching of the crisp top layer of snow beneath her feet echoed into the silence of the frigid night air, fighting only with the sound of the waves for attention. Above her, a cloudless sky was filled with stars that sparkled like the most valuable of jewels. The half-moon's light blanketed the snow around the area in a silvery glow and added to the brightness.

For a winter's night, it was milder than they usually had here. Katla sought out the corner and nodded to the guard standing a short distance away from her. This was not the first time she'd come here to sort out her thoughts or to spend some time away from everyone else, so this guard nodded and walked a few paces away to give her the area to herself. Only then did she let go of the tightness in her body and breathe slowly. The coldness made her shiver as she inhaled through her nose, so she pulled the hood of her cloak up and tugged the collar close to warm the chill before breathing in again.

If what her father had arranged stood, she would be leaving here for ever in just weeks. As eldest daughter and heir to her mother, she'd always thought she would remain here and care for the lands of her birth. The perfect place for the half-Pict, half-Norse daughter who had been bred and raised here. Trained to care for those in the village and the castle. Skilled in healing and sewing and knowledgeable in overseeing livestock and people.

Then her father arranged her first marriage, at her stepmother's behest, to a Norseman, disregarding any respect he had for the local customs or people. Or any promises he'd made to her mother. She'd been sent north to her father's lands and lived there during her short marriage, returning to her family and duties here after her husband's untimely yet welcome death.

Now, it would all begin again.

Katla eased the hood back as she stared out at the sea that would soon carry her northwards to live in her stepmother's holdings. Though Kolga's son from her first marriage held the Kingship that had passed from Kolga's father, everyone understood who truly ruled those lands. King Harald had been hesitant to grant Eithr the Kingship until her father, Thorfinn, stood surety for him. Her father had never explained, and indeed would never admit it, but Katla suspected that Kolga's marriage to her father was nothing more than part of a larger plan to claim that throne for her son.

But why? Why would her father do that? He was a nobleman in his own right, sworn to King Harald and the holder of his own lands in the north as well as those here through her mother's legacy. He had no need of this marriage. It had made little sense when it happened and made no sense now.

Yet her own marriage—if it happened—would tie him even more tightly to Kolga. An alliance like this, marrying the daughter of a powerful and wealthy Norse jarl, would give Arni stature and connections that he would never have earned or received otherwise. And since he was not connected by kith or kin, other than his position as Kolga's commander, such a match as this was unexpected.

The noise of someone's approach pulled her from her thoughts. Katla turned to find Enfreth walking towards her. At this moment, she had nothing to say to this man. From the pity in his gaze, it was clear he'd known about her father's plans and never revealed anything to her. Enfreth had known her from her birth until this day, through every good time and bad in her life, and his lack of loyalty pierced her deeply. Katla turned her gaze back to the sea and waited for him to speak.

'Katla,' he began. 'My lady, your father wishes to speak to you. In his chambers.'

She nodded without looking at him and waited for him to leave. A moment—or several of them—would be needed to prepare herself to face her father and she wanted the peace of this place for that. When she heard no sound of his retreat, she spoke.

'You may go.'

'Your father...'

'I will seek him out. You may go.'

'My lady, I would explain if you would permit it,' he said. Pity filled his voice now and she could not bear it. She turned and walked to the steps. He reached out and touched her arm, drawing back when she shuddered. 'I pray you to hear me.'

'On the morrow, Enfreth.' She shook her head in reply and drew her arm away. Then Katla walked until she reached the door and stopped to gather herself before facing her father.

She'd been the obedient daughter, had she not? She had smiled and accepted his words and the abominable marriage he'd arranged. She'd not, by word or deed, shown anyone her displeasure over the matter. Though several who'd been present could read her face better than most, she'd acquiesced to her father in front of their people.

He could not be angry at her. He could not find fault in her behaviour. He could not. So why then, as she took the last steps that placed her before his chamber, did her heart race and her palms sweat? A ridiculous question, really, since she knew the answer—she knew from recent experience to expect the worst.

Lifting her hand, she knocked on the chamber's door and waited to be called in. For the first time in a long time, she found her father alone. She closed the door behind her and stood with her hands clasped within her cloak and waited. He motioned her to the chair next to the table and she sat. At least he could not see her hands trembling.

'I know you were surprised by the announcement,' he said. 'It has been planned for a while, but I thought it best to wait before it was known.'

'Why?' she asked quietly.

'Why?' He frowned at her. 'Why have you worry over it for weeks, months even, when nothing could be done.'

'Nay, Father. Why? Why him? Why me? Why?' If a pleading tone filled her voice, she could not help it.

She would fall to her knees and beg if that would help her in this matter. 'Why are you doing this to me?'

He shoved back in a sudden move and his chair crashed to the floor behind him. Katla prepared herself as best she could for the coming blows. He strode around the table between them and stood over her, clenching his fists as rage poured off him.

This would be bad. Truly bad. When, in spite of his heavy breathing, he did not strike her, she dared a look at him. Pity? He looked on her with something that she thought was pity. Then, the customary anger was back and she waited for his hand.

'There is much you do not know,' he whispered. Katla looked up at him once more and found him staring back at her. His face aged years in that moment and he appeared tired and worn, too. 'Much you cannot and will not ever know.'

He lifted his hand and she tried not to flinch. Instead of hitting her, he dragged it through his hair and then rubbed his face. When he dropped it to his side and stepped back, Katla was stunned.

'You must marry this man, Katla. When Kolga comes, when the seas open once more, he will come to take you north to be his wife.' Before she could think of words to say, he nodded at the door. 'You may go.'

Katla stood then and did not wait for her legs to steady beneath her before leaving. At his dismissal, all the questions that filled her thoughts fled as she did the same. Even with so many things she wished to say and so many questions unanswered, she ran. She must look like the veriest coward as she scampered towards the door, but she cared not. When her hand touched the latch, her father spoke her name.

'Katla.' He stared at her for a moment. 'I am sorry.'

Nothing else. Not that she expected warmth or caring from him, but, no explanation beyond that? He turned then and walked to the small window and stared out of it, dismissing her from his attention, leaving her stunned and confused.

She left his chamber without thinking about a destination. She could go back to the walls and try to sort out this whole mess. She could go to her chambers and try to find rest. How long she wandered, she knew not. When Katla stopped before a door, she realised her feet had brought her to a place she had no reason to be. A place that could not give her the answers she needed or wanted.

Katla stood before the prisoner's cell without knowing why she came here. What could Brandt Sigurdsson do for her? Why had she come here?

'Is someone there?' His deep voice echoed from within.

Part of her wanted to leave without saying a word. He had no place in her life and she had no reason to be here. And yet, he knew her father and had known him for many years. Even before Kolga entered his life. She'd heard her father say that Brandt had saved his life in a battle.

Could he tell her more about her father than she knew?

But, could she trust him? He was her father's enemy

and he faced death at the hands of the King. Why would he tell her the truth of what he knew?

'I can hear your breathing out there.'

Katla held her breath then, uncertain of what to do. What good would knowing do her? The arrangement would still stand. Nothing would change that if her father supported it. She turned then to leave when his words stopped her.

'What brings you here in the dark of the night, Katla Thorfinnsdottir?'

The sounds of the chains moving warned her of his approach towards the door. Katla moved away from the opening in the door, still undecided about speaking to him.

'What has put the fear into you this night, Katla?' The chains rattled. 'What brought you to my door?'

She stood in silence and waited for what he would say next, trying all the while to calm her breaths and to control the ever-present fear that ruled her life. Katla had almost chosen to leave when he spoke.

'I owe you my life, Katla. One I have decided to claim. If you have need of me, just say so.'

Why did she not fear him? Why did she want to accept his offer of help? Katla could not explain it, but it was true. She turned and stepped in front of the opening in the door.

'My father. I would speak to you about my father.'

Chapter Six

Brandt stood in the darkness of the cell, trying not to hear the need and fear in her voice. And, in spite of his resolve to remain unmoved, he could not. For now, he would blame his weakness on the debt he owed her and sort out the rest later.

'What do you wish to know about your father?' He took the last step that he could on the leash of the chains and waited. She stood outside the door, but he could not see her in the shadows. 'Do you think I will tell you the truth?' In that next moment, from the way those shadows shifted in front of the torch left burning in the corridor, he knew she'd moved in front of the small opening in the door. 'I am an outlaw. A criminal. A man facing death.'

'Tell me of my father's debt to you. The one that made him spare your life.' So, she would ignore his taunting question. 'I pray you.' Her last words were whispered so softly, he may have imagined them.

Brandt let out a breath that filled the space before

him with a fog of heat. He did not wish to speak of the Thorfinn he'd known before his crime. The man of honour he'd grown up with who could never have planned to murder Brandt's family. He needed to hold on to his righteous rage to see this through. To see to the justice his dead kith and kin demanded from the grave and beyond. And if he needed to think of the lovely Katla Thorfinnsdottir as an enemy to keep his wits about him, he would.

'It makes no difference now. His debt is paid and I am free of it as well.'

'Do you plan to kill him, then?' she asked.

He blew out an angry breath and tried to move closer to the door. The chains rattled loudly in the silence and she startled, shifting back a pace as though he could get to her.

'Aye.' Brandt nodded his head and stared towards the wall. 'He deserves to die for what he has done.'

'So, why did you save him before?' She'd ignored his taunt about her father's present crimes in favour of a story from years before. Strange.

'Do you always dig at the past this way, Thorfinn's daughter? Will you not let it go?'

'I will if you will,' she said.

He leaned his head back and laughed then. It was hard to hold his anger in place when she surprised him so. At times, she was filled with fear. At other times, her words showed her to be intelligent and bold. Could it hurt to tell her of her father's past? Mayhap he would see something he'd missed if he told her the story?

Mayhap the reason behind Thorfinn's betrayal lay in their shared past?

'You may regret this bargain, Thorfinn's daughter,' he warned.

'I am certain that I will, Sigurd's son. But I have learned to live past my regrets.'

He was glad of the darkness then, for her words stunned him. It exposed more about this enigmatic young woman who could hold the answers he needed. A chill that had nothing to do with the frigid air around him teased down his spine as he understood that she presented a danger of a different kind to him and to his survival.

'Your father and mine were allies once. They fought against a common enemy on the King's behalf many times.' He relaxed his hands and stopped fighting the chains. 'About six years ago, we rode out on the King's orders, seeking out a renegade who'd killed a number of traders in one of the coastal villages.' Brandt could see in his thoughts the small town where they hunted the outlaw Snorri Ruriksson down. Remembering the scene, Brandt could almost smell the stench of death and fire as the trapped men began to burn down everything around them to avoid being caught.

'Were you alone? The only ones sent?' she asked. He could see her head through the opening of the door. She'd moved closer once more.

'Nay, six of us were sent. Your father was in charge.' Brandt shifted and then moved back to the pallet and sat. 'We had no idea that Snorri had prepared for our arrival. I followed your father down an alley and we walked into an ambush.'

Katla inhaled as though she would speak then, but didn't say a word.

'He was knocked to the ground while I took on two men. I fought them and when I finally overcame them, I saw Thorfinn was unconscious. I stumbled over and managed to fight off another who had his sword aimed at your father. Then I dragged Thorfinn back to where our men were gathered and he recovered before we finished Snorri off.' Brandt remembered that day and the two long scars he wore from the final assault.

And he remembered the time when Thorfinn had been a friend, an honourable man who had fought at his side. Brandt's mouth soured at such memories now. That same man and his wife, Brandt's own aunt, had brought about the destruction of his father and many others in their family. He spat into the corner to rid himself of the bitter taste of betrayal that burned him.

He glanced towards the flickers of light from the torch outside the door, just waiting for the first question to spring from her lips. He did not doubt she had many to ask. He began to count the moments as he waited. He'd barely reached five when she spoke.

'That was six years ago?'

'Aye. Just before winter's grasp took hold. Did he tell you of it when he came back here? The story was told many times in our hall for he went on to kill Snorri himself in spite of being injured.'

'Nay. My father speaks little of such matters to me.

And to admit an honour debt such as that one would have embarrassed him.'

'Better to have a debt owed than to have died in that fight,' he offered. By the gods, he hated how admiration for the man entered his voice then! Brandt wanted to hate the man behind the destruction of his family and yet something just did not feel right about this. He'd been an ally and a friend for many years before turning his back on them.

Oh, his brothers had gathered all the evidence and followed it to discover who was behind the plot and it pointed to Thorfinn and Kolga, Brandt's aunt. The items used to bribe and pay the killers could be traced back to them. The attempts on Sandulf's life on Thorfinn's ship. And more that pointed directly at Katla's father and her stepmother. Brandt did not doubt for a moment Thorfinn's involvement. Damn, but her questions had made him think on matters he did not wish to.

'So, are you satisfied now that I have told you what you asked?' She'd gone quiet where she stood outside the door.

'Aye.'

One word was all she said. But she did not move away from the door yet. She was not done. That much he could tell. Something was bothering her. Something she thought he could help her with. Strange that, asking a man who had come to kill her father for help. Brandt waited, counting the number of her breaths in the silence.

One. Two. Three. Four.

As he waited for the fifth one, she shuffled and

turned and began walking down the corridor. Brandt discovered that, in spite of their situations, in spite of being enemies, he did not want her to go in such a state. Her pain and confusion had screamed out with every word and every breath and he wanted... He wanted...

To make it go away.

Gods almighty, he wanted to make it stop as she had made his pain stop. This unwanted strong need to keep her close and talking forced the words from him.

'Before you go...' he said. When he heard her pause, he spoke once more. 'My thanks for the buckets of water.'

'They arrived? Good.' Katla came back to the opening and Brandt let out a breath. She ran this household, so why did she not know her orders had been followed? Something had distracted her. Something bothered her; even now it filled her thoughts, for he could almost hear her turning over every word he'd spoken to her about her father.

'Aye. The one of hot water was a welcome surprise. A prisoner never expects to have his comforts tended to.'

He'd been surprised when the guard opened the door and three buckets of fresh water were brought in. To find a bowl of soap and one bucket filled with water hot enough to scald his skin was unexpected at best. He'd been able to wash not only his body, but also his head and hair with the amount of water provided.

'So, my thanks to you, Katla Thorfinnsdottir.'

'I am...' she started. He only heard the released breath instead of more words. 'Glad.'

'How long has it been since I arrived here? Can you tell me the date?' he asked. 'I know the days are lengthening once more, but I know not how long until the spring thaw.'

''Tis midmonth now, January. Ships should sail back and forth on the seas in but six weeks or so.' He could not see her, but he could hear her.

'So, I have been here a month? Those first weeks are lost to me in a haze of fever and pain,' he admitted. 'Still, I owe my life to you for your care during them. No matter if I face execution in six weeks or not.'

She gasped then and ran, the sound of her footsteps moving quickly away down the corridor until he heard the outer door slam behind her.

He was the one facing certain death, even if it was one he both sought and expected. Killing Thorfinn in battle in his best condition would be difficult, but Brandt was no match for the seasoned and successful warrior in the condition he was now. So, Katla's reaction was puzzling to him. Was she so soft-hearted that she worried about his death? Nay, something else was at play here with her and it was something that distressed her.

This encounter confused him in so many ways. She'd sought him out to speak about her father—the one person he wished not to speak about. She'd made him remember the good times in his life when her father had been his friend, his mentor even, in the times when his own father's harsh behaviour and attitudes had worn Brandt down. Much like Hafr had served as guide to his younger brother Alarr. And as Joarr had done with him and his brothers.

Pulling against the chains, he growled out his frustration. He had not planned to live through his attempt to seize justice in his challenge with Thorfinn. Thinking of their common pasts distracted Brandt from his anger. And his plan, such as it was.

He'd had no doubt that Thorfinn's men would finish him off after or even kill him before, so to be alive at his enemy's word was not what he'd thought would happen. He would still challenge Thorfinn before the King when he was taken there—if he got the chance to do so. Having been declared an outlaw, even one taken before the King, he may never be permitted to speak before Harald, but he had sworn to his brothers that he would try. His most recent realisation, made just this day as he sat in the dark, cold prison room, was that if he wished to have a sliver of hope in succeeding against Thorfinn or anyone else, he needed his strength back.

Six weeks? Not very long to train, especially not in his circumstances. Brandt glanced around the chamber and saw nothing that he could use. He had only a pallet in the corner, a stool, a bucket of water and another for necessities. The chains were his constant leash. The chains…

Brandt stood facing the wall at the full distance the chains would allow him. They slid through an iron ring and he could pull in one direction then the other to stretch his arms, one after the other. So he did exactly that and the sounds of the iron links sliding back and forth through the ring filled the chamber and gradually fell into a rhythmic pattern. He continued until his shoulders and arms struggled to keep the movements smooth. Until his muscles hurt.

Releasing his hold on the chains, he sat on the edge of the pallet, surprised by the effort it had taken. The exertion, even as limited as it had been, took his breath away and made his arms, his back and his shoulders cramp. And yet it felt good. Good to work his body for the first time since he had nearly died. Winded and exhausted, he searched the chamber for other things he could use to train with and could find naught.

That would be his first task, then. Well, the first after he rid himself of the chains. Then he must devise ways to regain his strength so that his battle, if he got one, would be a success and he could reclaim the honour of his father and those who had died.

When the door to his cell was thrown open at first light, Brandt discovered that someone had given him exactly the opportunity he needed, if he could survive it.

A decision had been made that he should not languish in the cell after all, but be used for manual labour. Brandt fought the urge to laugh as he was dragged outside into the frigid, but clear and crisp, winter's day. He inhaled deeply and would swear the smell of the freshness improved his condition immediately. The dank odours of that underground chamber were soon replaced with ones very similar to his home—snow, cold, fresh winds and even the salty scent of the nearby sea. He pulled in several deep breaths then to fill his lungs and stood still to allow the cold winds to blow away the smells of the dungeon.

The strange excitement that filled him did not last long as his deplorable physical condition was proven almost with the first task given him. A wall to one of the outbuildings in the yard near the keep had crumbled and the rocks and rubble needed to be cleaned away so that the wall could be repaired. Within a very short time, Brandt had to suffer the mocking and laughter of those who guarded him and watched his struggle. Several times he battled the temptation to fight back and use the chains on his wrists to pay them back for their taunts and insults.

Soon, he ignored them for he needed every bit of concentration to move to the next rock, bend and lift it and carry it away without falling over himself. His arms and shoulders and back screamed in pain with every movement he made. His legs shook with exhaustion with each step he took or if he crouched down to get a better grasp of the rock he needed to lift. More than once, he felt the ground beneath him begin to wobble and his vision cloud over. The guards laughed even louder as he nearly passed out several times that morn.

Only one man interrupted his work. Alfaran approached him and held out a skin to him. The guards were silent in their commander's presence and when he accepted it and lifted it to his mouth, Brandt tasted ale. After three mouthfuls, he returned it and nodded to the man. Soon after that, the guards lost their taste for mockery and simply watched him in silence. One stood with his sword drawn and the other with an arrow nocked and ready should it be needed.

Again, he wanted to laugh at the ludicrous scene it must be—weapons readied to shoot him if he...ran? Fought back? Brandt was amused and, at the same time, ashamed that he could do neither. And he would not attempt to escape until he had his chance to claim justice.

His shame increased when he did collapse after a few hours of work and he had to be helped—dragged— back to his cell and thrown inside it. The laughter of the guards and those watching in the yard echoed behind him until his body gave out.

His last thought as he fell into the sleep of unconsciousness was that his plan was going well. So well, it would probably kill him.

Chapter Seven

$\mathcal{A}$t another time or if someone else was involved, Katla would never begrudge the men who protected and served her father their bit of rough play or fun. The behaviours of men had never not baffled her and, in spite of watching every possible one in her life here, she was confused about why this bit bothered her so much.

Mayhap it was the helpless man at the centre of it? Mayhap it was because Alfaran had instigated it? Mayhap because Brandt did not deserve to be humiliated as she had been so many times?

Katla shook herself from such thoughts and made her way to her chambers for her basket and herbs and then the kitchen for other supplies before heading down beneath the keep. She'd watched them drag him inside and, when he did not raise his head, she knew he was unconscious. No doubt he was in pain. He might have injured or torn the muscles she'd worked so hard to save. When she approached his chamber, arms filled with all sorts of supplies and medicaments, the guard blocked her way.

'I would see the prisoner,' she stated. When the man did not move, she tried to step around him. When that did not work, she stepped back and glared at him. 'Open the door, Geir.'

'Lady, I...' the young man began with hesitation.

'My father's orders are clear in this, Geir. I am in charge of the prisoner's care while he is here.' Still, the man did not move to obey and instead watched something over her shoulder. Someone.

'Why do you come here, Katla?' Alfaran stood behind her. His steps continued until she could feel his breath moving the air there. 'He is healed and will be used as the Jarl sees fit.'

All of her first responses to his words, or to his manner of treating and speaking to her in disrespect, faded away. Arguing with this man usually just made her angrier. He held power of a different kind than she did here. He could follow up his words with actions that could punish men for disobedience. He did not need to wait for her father to confirm any order he gave as she did. She controlled through her father while he controlled with her father.

That distinction had been made clear over and over again throughout her life and Alfaran relished in it, rubbing it in her face whenever he could. So, she had learned how *not* to deal with this man many years ago. The problem was that success in dealing with him was a finely balanced, narrow path filled with appeals to his masculinity, his loyalty and his fear of being replaced.

'Open the door, Geir. I wish to show Alfaran something,' she said in a quiet voice to the guard without facing Alfaran. The guard paused and waited on Alfaran's permission. Soon the door swung open and Geir stepped away. 'Hold the lantern up.' The man did so.

As she suspected, Brandt had been tossed on the floor there, left as he landed. She did not move to enter, but looked up at her father's commander.

'You want to work him. Can an unconscious man be worked? Look there,' she said as she pointed to the dark and growing stain on his breeches. 'His wounds bleed once more. If he bleeds to death, he cannot be worked. He cannot be taken north to stand trial or be punished by the King if he dies here. I heard my father's words, Alfaran. And I heard his displeasure when you nearly killed this man with your wilful ignorance. How will my father react if you kill him this time after he's warned you not to do so?'

She turned to face him, waiting for him to absorb her words, truly words of warning, and the knowledge that both of them knew about her father's wrath. 'So, may I see to the prisoner's wounds, Alfaran?'

Alfaran did not answer her directly. Instead, he looked past her to Geir and spoke. 'The Jarl's daughter is to continue seeing to the prisoner while he still lives and while she still lives here.'

Alfaran's gaze moved to hers then and she could see how happy he was that she would be leaving. That conniving, gloating, overbearing…! Her tongue would bleed before she spoke any of what she was thinking. She placed that blank, respectful expression on her face, the one she used to try to placate her father, and nodded.

'Geir, I will need that lantern inside.' Katla did not think her voice shook with the anger that filled her. She thought it calm and even. 'And I need your help placing him on the pallet there.' She and Geir were out of breath by the time they moved the massive man from the floor on to the pallet, removing the cloak tied around his neck and placing him on his side so she could reach the bleeding wound on his leg. 'The chains. Remove them, so I can move his arms.'

'But, lady—' Geir began. She stopped him with a glare.

'Has he moved on his own, Geir? Has he opened his eyes or made a sound? Nay, he has not. He is no danger to me in this condition.' She leaned back from her kneeling position next to Brandt and sat on her heels. 'I pray you, remove the chains.'

She almost pitied the young man, almost, as he thought for a long moment about whether or not to obey her in this. He even glanced at the door as though deciding if he should seek out his commander for approval. Then, with a shrug, he unlocked the chains.

'I will be outside if you need help, lady,' he said as he pulled the door closed. She waited for the sound of the key turning in the lock and his steps away from the cell before reaching for her basket.

If truth be told, she worried over Brandt's lack of response. When she finally cut away the fabric of the breeches and poked and prodded the wound that had reopened on his leg, Brandt did not moan or even startle. At a loss over what to do, she tended the bleeding wound, stitched it anew and spread an unguent before bandaging it. She did not realise he'd awakened until he laughed. A hoarse, weak one, but a welcome sign he was not dying.

'I can only hope your words are not about me,' he whispered.

'You're awake. Thank the gods! What were you thinking?' she asked, keeping her voice low so Geir could not hear. Brandt shifted then, moaning as he moved his arms and shifted on the pallet. When he slid a hand down to examine the wound, she pushed it away. 'Do not undo my work again, Brandt.'

'I assure you that I did not do this to vex you, Katla. Or to undo your previous stitchery.' He tried to move then, but stopped and lay still. 'Or to stir your wrath against me. 'Twas not my choice to feel as though I've been trampled by my horse and my brothers' as well.'

She tried not to smile at him. Clearly he was in pain, the new stitches must pull the already tender skin and he had been pushed to labour hard in the yard before his collapse. Smiling seemed wrong and yet she could not help it.

'Only a fool would have wished such a thing.'

'I never thought you a fool, Brandt.'

'Did you not? I am sure you said those things to me when you sewed me up the first time.'

The heat of a blush crept up her cheeks as she remembered calling him, at the least, a fool for his arrival and challenge. She just had not thought he'd heard her in his condition.

'Well…'

'Just so,' he whispered. 'Your father apparently wishes to get his ultimate revenge by killing me and so he makes certain that I cannot fight him when we go before the King.'

Katla shrugged, for she had no idea if this was her father's plan or not. He was ruthless enough to do such a thing, but was he dishonourable enough to? If he had, as Brandt accused, been behind the murder of Brandt's kin, aye, he would be that dishonourable. The man whose life Brandt had saved six years ago would never stoop to this and yet that man had changed greatly since then.

She turned away and sought out her basket, searching for and finding the small bottle of tincture of poppy that would help his pain. Katla poured a cup of ale and then added a few drops of the potent ingredient. Too much and he would sleep too deeply. When she held it out to him, he viewed it with suspicion.

'Do you do his work here, Katla?' She couldn't help it then; she cursed aloud at him as she shoved the cup towards him.

'You addle-brained idiot! By the gods, I thought you were smarter than this!' She put the cup down and made fists with her hands that she so wanted to smash against his chest at his accusation. 'I could have ended your life so many times and I did not.' She raised a fist then, anger pulsing through her body as she spoke. 'Only a fool makes an enemy when they could have a friend. Only a fool insults the only person standing between death and life. Only a fool…' Katla clenched her jaws and screamed silently through them. When she dared to look at him, she found Brandt smiling at her. It just made her angrier, but he laughed then.

'You may hit me if you need to, Katla. Sometimes it can feel good to release that anger.' She startled at such words. Hitting never helped. Hitting was not good. Hitting… She glanced at him then.

'Ah. I beg your pardon for saying that,' he said. He studied her face and she knew that he knew the truth. 'I am certain that you will discover an appropriate way to punish me for my foolish behaviours when you are poking and prodding me again.'

He reached out to take the cup from her. It did not happen quickly, for it took him much effort and caused him much pain to simply lift his arm. Katla held it out to him and Brandt's gaze bore into hers as he tilted the cup and drank every drop down. Somehow, the intensity in his blue eyes as they reflected the flickering light of the lantern at his side told her that this was more than following her directions. It was a show of faith. A demonstration of trust.

He trusted her. With his life.

This Viking enemy showed her more consideration than her father or any other man had. Her throat grew tight at the realisation of it. It took an enemy's act to show her respect.

He faltered then, his arm shaking with the effort it took to hold the cup and his head fell back on the pallet as she grabbed the cup. She searched for the unguent in her basket and found it.

'If you could sit up, I could spread this on your arms and back. It will help the pain and the tightness.'

'Then I will,' he said.

Even his bold and quick agreement did not lessen the challenge of him changing position and getting his tunic off. He was out of breath and struggling to remain upright when he finished. Katla scooped some of the thick paste and rubbed it between her hands to warm it.

'By the gods, Katla! It smells like sh—' He turned his head and wrinkled his nose at the foul smell. She'd grown somewhat accustomed to it over the years of using it, but it did have a terrible odour. 'Will I smell like that, too?'

'All of your companions will complain about it.' Her dry words made him laugh then.

'I wish I'd had this at home. It would have made for a fitting trick on my brother,' he said. He let his head drop then and sat in silence as she massaged the ointment along his shoulders, tracing the fascinating shapes and colours imbedded in his skin. 'This would have spoiled Danr's fun with women. I wish I'd had it then...'

'Tell me of your brothers. You have four?' she asked. At first, he remained silent as the pain from her first touches on his aching arms nearly overwhelmed him. She could tell exactly when the unguent's ingredients started to ease it, too.

Brandt spoke then, sharing tales of himself and his four brothers as boys and then as young men and all the foolish things they'd done. At some moment in their conversation, he lifted his head and met her gaze as

they talked. She laughed quietly as some of the stories resembled the youthful foolishness that she and
Gemma had been guilty of at the same ages. Then she
noticed that he had not mentioned anything more recent about them.

'And your brothers? Where are they now?' Katla
felt the muscles beneath her fingers tighten then. Not
from pain.

'Here and there,' he said, turning his gaze from hers.
'Here and there.' Ah. He trusted her with his life, yet
not the lives of his brothers.

For a time, neither spoke. She continued to spread
the medicament down his arms, working it into his
skin as she went.

'I think we've met before this, Katla.'

'I do not remember.'

'I had about thirteen years at the time, I think. It is
hazy, being so long ago and with so much happening
since.' He searched her face then. 'You had about nine
or ten years then.'

Katla searched her own memories, trying to remember. 'Was it on my father's lands in the north?'

'Aye. A huge celebration was held that year to mark
the birth of the King's son and all those sworn to the
King—his Jarls and freemen and their families were
there. Sacrifices were made in honour of the gods' gift
to Harald. I remember two young blonde-haired girls
with Thorfinn.'

Being nine or ten years old felt like a lifetime ago to
her as she thought back on that journey and the mar-
vellous sights and sounds and foods and people. Her

mother had been alive then and her smile and laughter had lit up any gathering. No matter how much she tried, she could not remember meeting Brandt or his brothers. She'd met his father several times during his journeys here to visit her father.

Once, there had been talk of a match between their families, but her father had said he would honour her mother's wish for a man from Katanes for her eldest daughter. And there would be time enough to discuss Gemma's future.

There would be time enough.

Except things had changed and time had flown by, never allowing those discussions. Mother died. Katla was married off to Trygg. Father married Kolga. Now Katla would be married off once more before Gemma met her own fate. And once she was gone from here, she could do nothing more to protect her sister as she'd sworn to do. When she realised Brandt was watching her, she smiled and shook her head.

'I fear not. 'Twas so many years ago and I was astounded by the journey and the sheer size of it all. My mother preferred us to remain here, so it was an amazing thing to see the King and everyone. Yet I remember so little of it other than the feelings of being overwhelmed and happy.' Except for her mother's smile and laughter.

'That may be a good thing,' he said. 'I was quite an idiot at that age and did stupid things. I am glad you do not remember me then.'

In that moment, she wished for nothing more than to remember meeting him. To see him at that age before the tragedy had torn his world and family apart and put the hardness and bleakness in his eyes. To see him on the edge of manhood surrounded by four brothers.

'As most boys are.' She laughed then and could not help but tease him a bit. 'But look at you now. All grown up and not doing stupid things at all.'

He blinked once, then again before laughing. That he accepted her attempt at humour filled her with warmth and it felt good. After wiping her hands on a cloth to remove the remnants of the ointment, she handed him his tunic.

'So much for the good work of that hot water,' he said, sniffing as he slowly pulled the tunic over his head. 'But that lotion helped and I thank you for it.' He tugged on his shirt and then rotated his shoulders. 'Much better.'

'The tonic should help, too. It will not render you senseless, but will ease the pain.'

'I thought you had just accused me of having no sense, Katla.' He yawned then and settled back on the pallet.

'Just so.'

For a moment, watching his face in the soft light of the lantern as the drops of poppy took effect, she could imagine him before…everything. The masculine angles of his face, the lines of tightness around his mouth and eyes and the usual angry set of his mouth would have been happier. Softer. Gentler. That would have been the man his wife knew.

Had she, had Ingrid the wife he cried out to in his fevered dreams, loved him as much as he'd loved her?

Katla shook herself to rid the strange thought and gathered her supplies and packed them away in her basket. She stood, stretching as was her custom after such work, and turned to go. Geir had not returned to let her out, so she raised up on her toes and called his name out into the corridor.

'Do you know why your father has not come here to speak to me?' Brandt asked. She shook her head and shrugged.

'In all candour, I would have thought he would have come as soon as you were able to speak.' She turned back to the door as she heard Geir's approach.

'Ask him to come. I would speak to him.'

Katla faced him once more. 'Are you certain that is wise? If you anger him, your conditions here could be made worse.'

'He might speak to me of things in private that he would not in front of others.'

As Geir turned the key, Katla thought on his words and her most recent conversation with her father when she sought the reasons behind her coming marriage. In spite of her pleas, he'd revealed nothing. And she couldn't imagine that Brandt would plead for anything.

'I will tell him of your request. But, Brandt, think you this will end well?'

'None of this is going to end well, Katla. But I want to understand why my family was slaughtered and why I now face my own death. If he is behind it all, I want to know why. Why did he turn him from ally and friend into enemy? Just why.'

He would never know how closely his words echoed

her own. Would her father respond differently to this man's, this warrior's, this ally's, questions than he did to hers? He respected Brandt more, that much she could see in the way he had been spared and kept alive. So, mayhap Brandt would get his answers?

Geir pulled the door open and allowed her to pass. She made her way back to the hall and to the duties that waited for her there.

With a little more than a month before her departure, she worked with the servants and those who oversaw the day-to-day running of her father's lands here. Gemma was too young and inexperienced to take over the duties that had been Katla's since her mother's passing.

In making her way from task to task, she did not miss the close scrutiny of Alfaran. His dark stares and menacing glare did little to put her at ease. In the matter of Brandt Sigurdsson, Alfaran seemed to be opposed to the way her father chose to honour his own debt to the Norseman. As she passed him on her way to see her aunt, he whispered something under his breath. She turned back to face him, but he'd already moved away.

No matter that she did not hear the words he'd spoken, the tone had been filled with such malice that chills spread over her body and a trickle of fear inched its way through her, making her stumble then. His dislike of her position had always been obvious, but the words he'd uttered were more hateful than disrespectful.

She glanced around the hall to see if anyone else had heard him or noted his expression. No one was near enough, so she continued on to find her aunt.

And she knew that, at some time, she would pass along Brandt's request to her father. But the when and the how of that was something she must think on carefully. With each step she took, Katla felt like traps were set hidden beneath her feet. One wrong step, one trap sprung, could be dangerous to her and her sister.

Chapter Eight

Even though the exhaustion and the effects of the poppy draught Katla had given him pulled him towards sleep, Brandt could not sink into its oblivion. Instead of easing the tension in his body with her soft touch and strenuous massage, his body felt on fire. And when she had leaned against him, her full breasts pressing on his back or against his arm could not be ignored.

But, all that aside, what kept him awake was the realisation that he wanted her.

Oh, he had not been celibate, as Danr had, since the death of his family and Ingrid. He'd sated his needs with a woman here or there, but that was all he'd felt—an itch that needed scratching. What shivered through him was something very different. Something much more dangerous than anything he'd faced in his quest for justice.

Not only did he want Katla, he liked her as well. Worse, he wanted and liked her too much given that they were the son and daughter of bitter enemies and naught good could come from it for either of them. He laughed then, accepting the ludicrous idea of it. Yet he was just a man and she was a beautiful, intelligent woman with a lush body and a dry sense of humour that he appreciated. Not even the harsh treatment she'd been the recipient of had broken her spirit.

He admired her for that, too, damn him, and for her skills and her relentless drive to save his life, in spite of what that would mean in her own life if he succeeded.

No, this sudden desire for her could not end well if he acted on it. So, he would fight the way his body reacted when she worried her plump lower lip as she mixed this or that concoction. Or when she spread something warm on his skin. Or when she used just the tip of one finger to glide over the colourful designs imbedded on his chest or shoulders and the old scars of past battles. And he would fight off any urges when she slid her hands over the injuries on his thigh, checking for bleeding.

Gods! But he was tempted to tear out the new stitches to be able to savour her caresses so close to his cock. If she slipped, if her movements shifted, if she touched him as he'd like...

The aroused part of him reared now and Brandt reached down and wrapped his hand around it. He must be feeling better if the needs of the flesh had returned. As he sought relief, he could see her face before him. The way her mouth moved as she worked. He could hear the harsh curses she whispered in a breathless voice as she saw to his injuries. He could almost imagine her strong fingers in place of his own, stroking his flesh until…he found release.

That night passed slowly for him. His dreams took him back to his younger years, when he and his brothers ran wild in their village. To happier days when his family gathered in their longhouse to celebrate a feast or a good harvest. Sitting in a place of honour at his father's side. As though watching someone else, Brandt could see the streak of pride and arrogance in his own expression. He could see all the possibilities of what could come and what would come.

And there, impossibly in his father's hall, stood Katla watching him, too. She looked just as he'd remembered, or thought he'd remembered when he'd asked her if they'd met. A young girl on the edge of womanhood, a beauty in the making with her long blonde tresses that swirled around hips that would fill out into the curves of a siren.

Then he relived all sorts of times and places in his life—good ones and bad—and the grown Katla watched. She watched as he married Ingrid, as he fought alongside his father and with those who'd mentored him and even as he'd burned and buried his father and his wife. She stared at him with no guile or guilt, just open curiosity as his life passed in those dreams. And when the banging on his door woke him in the still, dark morning, he half expected to see her standing there.

'Twas not her.

* * *

He was chained once more and led outside for another day of hard work and he saw or heard little in paying heed to his every step that morning. When a terrible storm moved in, with slashing rains and winds strong enough to knock men off their feet, he was taken inside to one of the storage cellars and made to move barrels. No one spoke to him other than to give him orders and, this day, no one mocked him. Though the labour took all he had, they did not push him beyond his endurance.

When he was done, they dragged him through the hall and Brandt searched for any sign of Thorfinn or his daughter. Neither one could be seen, though he had little enough time to look. And though Katla did not visit his prison cell, buckets of water and a huge bowl of a thick and fragrant stew did arrive. As he ached his way to sleep that night, he thought he might have given up both of those for her presence.

The hard work each day followed by a hearty meal and hot water became his routine over the next several days. By the third day, he did not hurt as much. His arms and shoulders were becoming accustomed to the lifting and pulling and the wounds seemed completely healed. The one that Katla had most recently stitched did not bleed again, which pleased him and yet disappointed him at the same time.

He laughed each time he caught himself holding his breath and listening to every step that came down the corridor towards his door. The once brave and fearless

and arrogant Brandt Sigurdsson was reduced to a pitiful prisoner waiting on the benevolence of his enemy's
daughter. The sensible part of him—one he did have in
spite of Katla's claim of the opposite—knew that more
time spent with her would simply make things worse.

He could never have her. From the way in which she
flinched during any approach, she would never have
him. Or, he suspected, any man if she could choose
that. She had a kind heart and her actions demonstrated
that. And, in this search to reclaim his family's honour,
he would not sink so low as to take advantage of her
kindness. He'd sworn not to harm her and he would not.

That didn't mean he didn't want to. That didn't mean
his traitorous, unruly flesh did not crave her every
touch.

He lay on his pallet far into the long dark hours of
the night and thought on the proof he and his brothers
had collected so far in their search for those who'd arranged for the deaths of so many kith and kin. It had
been more than two years since they'd begun their
quest for the truth of it all and more than three since
Alarr's wedding when it all began.

Alarr, who'd been grievously wounded at his wedding as the massacre began, discovered that Feann,
King of Éireann, had played no part in the murders,
though not for lack of wanting to. In discovering that,
a bond between the King and Brandt's half-brothers
Rurik and Danr had been revealed. Rurik had followed
clues to Northumbria and uncovered a pendant belong-
ing to their mother among the belongings of one of the
assassins hired to carry out the plot.

After Brandt had wrongly threatened his youngest brother for not protecting Ingrid while he himself rode north at his father's bidding, Sandulf had travelled to Constantinople. Attempts were made to kill him, on Thorfinn's own ship, but Sandulf found two more of their mother's pendants, leading them all to believe she was involved. But the worst thing was when Sandulf gave him Ingrid's two necklaces—one Valkyrie figure given to her by his father and the other the half of Thor's hammer that Brandt himself had given to her.

If he'd lost his mind when she was murdered, he lost the last bit of his heart when Sandulf handed that to him. Found amid the belongings of the man who'd killed her, it was the only thing precious he had left of her. Now, safely hidden outside Wik Castle, it would add to the burden of proof they'd collected that pointed not at his mother, but at his Aunt Kolga and her second husband, Thorfinn.

Yet, even as he examined the evidence that pointed to the man whose prisoner he was, Brandt found he could still not reconcile it. His aunt's connection? Oh, aye, that was easy enough to understand. His father had seized control over Maerr when he married the younger sister, in defiance and in complete disregard of the elder sister's claim to it from her father.

His father had been an arrogant, ruthless arse who had pursued his own interests and ignored everyone else's. That he had enemies who wanted him dead was no surprise at all. But the virulence of the attack was.

If their suspicions were correct, their aunt had planned it all and carried it out with the help and back-

ing of her husband. The one who owned the ship where
Sandulf had nearly died and where their father's true
assassin had. The one who had stood before Harald to
take control of the Kingship of Maerr, and its wealth
and people, for Kolga's pitiful son. The man whose
prisoner he now was.

So, what chance did Brandt have of even making it
to Maerr to challenge Thorfinn? If Kolga and Thorfinn had killed so many and hidden their involvement
from sight, would they even allow him to live to make
the journey north? Although Thorfinn had paid back
his honour debt, which still confounded Brandt, why
let him continue to survive to make his claim?

Though his father had made many enemies, he also
had allies. Powerful men who would stand up and back
Sigurd's sons if proof was presented. Brandt was so lost
in his thoughts, examining the evidence he'd brought
with him to Katanes and trying to sort out a way forward, that he never heard the footsteps down the corridor or the arrival of someone outside the door.

As though his thoughts had conjured up the man,
Thorfinn Bjornsson turned the key and entered.

He'd fought the urge to speak to Brandt since the
day he'd walked up to Wik Castle and challenged him.
And he admitted to himself that it was fear that had
kept him from doing so.

Until now.

Soon, his wife would return and take Katla north
to marry her commander. Soon, his sin of wilful ignorance would come home to roost, now that he had as

many questions as Sigurd's son probably had. He realised that he needed the knowledge that Brandt and his brothers might have in order to take control of the situation that now spun like a maelstrom through his life. A maelstrom that would destroy everything if Thorfinn did not find a way to slow it down or avoid it altogether.

And yet, he could admit to nothing. Would not admit or even acknowledge any claims made by his friend's sons or those who supported them. As he should have. As he would have, had not...

There would be time enough for regrets later. He stood in the doorway as Brandt finally saw him and sat up on the pallet in the corner. The young man made no attempt to rise, he just stared as though Thorfinn was an apparition. A ghost appearing in the dark. And that was how Thorfinn felt, a man disappearing from the life he'd had.

'Why?' The one word echoed to him from the shadows. Was that not exactly what Katla had asked? 'Just tell me why, Thorfinn.'

'Why did I stand before the King and not defend your father when he was accused of treachery? That is truly what you wish to know, is it not?' Brandt stood then, but did not take a step.

'What treachery? What proof that my father plotted against Harald?' Brandt stopped and blew out air from his chest like a winded horse. 'How could...? Why would a man who'd stood at his side in life and in battle stand before the King and lie?' Brandt took one step, then backed up. 'Did taking my father's place in Maerr bring you riches enough so you would sell your honour? Did you get the power that you crave by betraying him? Us? By killing my wife and son?'

Thorfinn grimaced then, still appalled by the deaths involved in this. If only he had reacted differently to the threat, all of this would have... With a shake of his head, he shrugged. 'You do not understand, Brandt. So much you do not know.'

'Much that I do know, you mean? I know that Kolga had been extorting my mother and used the jewellery she got to pay the assassins who killed my wife. I know others were involved and they killed Sigurd. I know that my brother was attacked and nearly killed on your ship after Kolga promised him safe passage to Constantinople. I know that she could not have done this alone, that a man of means and power would have had to help her carry out her plot. I know that you have benefitted the most from my father's downfall, Thorfinn.'

Anger rose in Brandt's voice and each accusation grew louder and stronger. By the gods, the brothers had learned much more than Thorfinn had thought they could or would! Brandt knew the basics without realising it. Now, watching the fury build in the younger warrior, Thorfinn waited for him to attack. Yet, he did not. He stood in place, never threatening violence even as he struck blows with his words. Blows that were more dangerous than the young man knew.

Thorfinn suddenly felt much older than his years. Weaker than his strength and more and more certain that he would find no way out of this situation. More would die. His dau—Katla would suffer the most and it seemed he could do nothing to stop it all. That was another mistake he'd made, another weakness being exploited by his wife.

Was that why he'd insisted that Brandt be kept alive? Did he harbour some hope deep within that this man could do what he himself could not? Thorfinn let out a breath and turned away to leave. He'd learned at least one thing he had not known before and that might help him find out more.

'Is that your answer then, Thorfinn? Turn your back in silence and walk away?'

''Tis the only answer I have for you, Brandt. The only one.' Locking the door, he offered his friend's son one thing, knowing it might be the only way out for each of them. 'I will face you in a fair fight before the King, if he allows it.'

Thorfinn walked away, clenching his jaws at the raw scream that followed him. He climbed the stairs and put the key back in its place for the guards' use. A glance around the hall told him that none had seen him and that the silence of the night still prevailed. He made his way back to his own chamber and found that sleep eluded him again as his thoughts filled with more questions than answers.

Unless he found a way out of this mess, one he'd had a hand in creating, all he'd worked for his whole life, all he held precious, would be for naught. And because of his first wife's betrayal, he would lose more than his honour.

On the morrow he would ask Katla to seek out more about Brandt's brothers and the evidence they'd collected. About what more he knew that he would never willingly share with Thorfinn himself. Brandt had soft-ened towards Katla. If using her to find out more would help him, Thorfinn would do it.

He regretted his angry treatment of her when she did not understand her role in this whole, hellish mess. 'Twas not her fault that she was a bastard and not his daughter. He'd sworn an oath before witnesses to Mod-wenna while she lay on her deathbed that he would protect her daughters. He'd thought they were his, but it turned out not to be true. The fact that she was in-stead the child of another man could weaken his claim here. And the knowledge of his hand in the matter of Katla's husband's death—a man who surely needed to die—was being used against him.

How long before everything fell apart?

Brandt howled out his pain and anger and the sound of it became a war cry in his quest for justice. He should have struck Thorfinn down as every instinct within him wanted to, but something had held him back. His infernal need to understand the man had robbed him of the opportunity to end it. He turned and punched the wall with his fist, hoping for some satisfaction in hitting *something* if he could not hit *someone*.

The pain that shot through his hand and down his whole arm did not ease his anger or satisfy the need to strike out at all. Instead, he pulled back and looked at the shredded skin on his knuckles. Cursing, he tore off a strip from the edge of the tunic he'd been given and wrapped it tightly around his hand to staunch the bleeding. Mayhap he was as senseless as Katla had accused after all?

He paced around the small chamber, trying to let go of the useless anger that filled his body and soul. That would not redeem his father's honour. That would not help him prove his innocence or prove his aunt and Thorfinn guilty. Nay, for to do those things he must survive, he must find out more about their plans and he must present that to Harald.

Or he must get their evidence and whatever he discovered back to his brothers and they would pursue what he could not attain. Danr and Rurik were nephews to the high King of Eireann and might be able to seek his help now that they had made their peace with him. Sandulf and Alarr had offered to stand at his side. They could carry on the fight to have their rightful honour and place restored...if he could not.

He would not be complacent any longer. If Katla was his only connection to the world outside this cell and within the household, then he would use her to learn what he needed to know. He would stand before the King—and Thorfinn—with as much evidence as possible.

And he only had weeks to do it.

Chapter Nine

Her father's instructions still ringing loudly in her head, Katla made her way down to the prisoner. She'd waited until the household was asleep, with the winds of yet another winter storm blowing outside and a warm fire to lull them to rest, before sneaking her way along the edge of the shadows of the hall. A key to the cell door had appeared in her chambers and she carried it hidden in her sleeve. What plagued her most was how her father thought she could accomplish his aims.

'Get him to talk. Pay heed to what he says about his brothers. Their proof. About me or your stepmother. Speak only to me of his words. Find out as much as you can by any means.'

She had been tempted to ask about these new orders, but experience had taught her over these last several years that it was better not to. From his devious gaze and strange abruptness while speaking to her, she suspected that her father had met with Brandt after all and whatever had happened bothered him. If she used his recent behaviour and appearance as a guide, she thought it must have been two nights prior, for he seemed restless and exhausted as though not sleeping well.

Katla did not bother with a lantern. She let her sight adjust to the torchlight before moving down the corridor at the bottom of the stairway. When she reached the door to Brandt's cell, she paused and stood in the silence, listening for any sign that he was asleep or awake. With the way her father's man had him working now, she did not doubt he needed his rest.

'What brings you to my door once again, Katla?' A gasp escaped as he startled her with his question.

'How did you know?' she asked.

'Yours are footsteps too light to be those of a man. And you are the only woman either bold enough or *senseless* enough to come here alone in the dark of the night.' She heard the emphasis on that word—one she'd previously used to insult him.

His voice grew stronger and she realised he stood in front of her with only the door separating them. She could barely see him standing in the darkness, but the sound of his breaths told her of his position.

'I think we established who was the senseless one between the two of us, Brandt.'

Though she dared to tease him, did she dare enter when he was so close to the door? Would he try to escape? Or use his size and strength against her since he was recovered and growing stronger each day? The fear rose quickly and she pushed it down as best she could.

She slid the key from where she'd hidden it in her sleeve. His laugh comforted her in a perplexing way.

'Why are you here? Do you wish me to speak of your father again?' As though he'd heard her thoughts, he moved back away from the door and stood next to his pallet. 'I have given you my word that you will come to no harm by my hands. If...' he paused then and she could almost hear the smile in his voice '...if you wish to enter rather than stand outside there.'

It was almost a challenge he issued to her. The sensible thing would be to remain outside. Nay, the truly sensible thing would be to return to her bed and let this go. Ignore her father's instructions while pretending to do otherwise. Who would tell him of her disobedience? She could weave together some bits of conversation to report to him and make up stories about his kin and his journey here. How would her father know if she spoke the truth or not?

Her father would not.

In place of his plan, she'd come up with one of her own—an incredible one of her own, one that involved Brandt and would rely on trust between them. To carry it out, she would need his help and co-operation. She would need him to risk his possible freedom to help her first. She chuckled then and realised she stood here frozen in place, talking all the while to herself. What must this Viking think of her!

'I have something to ask you and would prefer to come in to do it. Will you swear not to try to escape if I enter?'

Her question was not so much senseless as foolish

and dangerous. Prisoners tended to wish they would not remain where their lives and health were endangered. Yet he'd said otherwise. He'd said he wanted his opportunity for justice and that meant staying here to be taken to the King.

'Escaping to what, Katla? If I leave here, I forfeit my chance to reclaim my family's honour and to avenge those who have died.' His words confirmed what she already knew. He stepped closer, but his voice grew softer. 'Nay, I will not attempt to escape or harm you. So, enter as you wish, Thorfinn's daughter.'

She slipped the key in the lock and twisted it. Her hands shook as she tucked it back in her sleeve and pushed open the door. How was it that she did trust him? Katla held her breath as she walked in, even though she tried to appear calm and brave. After pushing the door closed, she walked to the stool in the corner and sat down while Brandt sat on the pallet. It was so dark here that she could hardly see even the outline of his body across the cell from her. Why had she thought not bringing the lantern was a good thing?

'I will return,' she said.

Katla rushed back into the corridor and worked the torch from its holder. Placing it in the holder outside his door, she went back in and found him as she'd left him. At least she could see him. And, whether a good idea or bad, she would see his reaction to her request. As she'd relinquished duty after duty to one or another who would remain here after she departed for the orth, she knew she could not marry Arni and go to live under her stepmother's dominion. No matter that

Kolga's son was being prepared to take over as King there, it was Kolga's household and lands, not even her father's, where she would live.

Until... Until she did not.

Though she never thought of herself as a brave person, she would not wait for her life to end under Arni's brutal hand. The decision she'd made in the middle of a recent sleepless night came from two choices—the first was to accept this arrangement or escape from it.

She could not accept it.

So, then the alternatives became—did she end her life herself or escape from the one planned for her?

Everything came back to Gemma. If she escaped, Gemma would be alone. If she ended her life, though she was not certain she had the strength or courage to carry out such an act, Gemma was alone. Even if she went north as Arni's wife, Gemma would be alone. Katla knew to the marrow of her bones that she would not and could not choose any path that left her sister behind and defenceless.

That certainty had brought her back to the plan she was considering, and it all depended on the man sitting across the small space, staring expectantly at her. Her father's enemy. Her enemy?

'I am here. You are here. The door is closed and we have privacy, Katla. What do you wish to say to me?' he asked. Had he sensed the importance of this already? For there was no levity or teasing in his voice. Even his expression was serious and almost forbidding.

'I have something to ask of you, Brandt.' She lost

her nerve then and sat in the silence, trying to sort out exactly how she should say this to him.

'So you have said.' Their gazes met and she could read nothing in his that would help her.

'This must be important, or it would not have you tongue-tied like this. If you were angry, you would be cursing me under your breath or aloud. If you were fearful, you would yet be standing outside that door and not sitting here, giving me the means to escape or take you prisoner. So, just tell me what you ask of me.'

'I need you to help me and my sister escape from Wik and from my father's plans.'

The words just came flowing out, awkward and strange and tumbling out into the space between them. Katla could not look at him then. She jumped to her feet and walked to the doorway, peering out through the opening. A glance over her shoulder told her that he did nothing but stare off into the corner.

'Did you forget that I am the prisoner here, Katla? Why would you ask this of me?'

She clasped her hands together to keep them from trembling before him and faced him once more. Seeking the arguments she'd put together in her thoughts before coming here, she began.'You asked me what was wrong some nights ago when I came asking about my father.' He nodded. 'My father had announced at supper that evening that I am to marry again. And leave Wik. My home. Again. He has agreed that I should marry Kolga's commander.'

'My aunt's commander?' He frowned then and she

could tell he was trying to remember who that was. 'Who?'

'Arni Gardarsson.' She shivered even speaking his name. 'I have said no to the man before, but he has gained my father's permission this time.'

Terror filled her then and she shuddered at what she knew he would do to her. Since he'd told her in such horrifying detail what his plan for her was that she had run and emptied her stomach from his words, Katla did not have to guess. Her knees buckled then and she would have fallen to the floor if Brandt had not moved to her side and scooped her up in his arms. He placed her on the pallet and stepped away without waiting. The heat coming off his skin, his naked chest, had only begun to warm her when he let her go, watching her as one did a wounded animal.

'Why would he give permission?' he asked. 'I did not know you'd been married before.'

They'd never spoken of her past. He'd seen the bruises her father had left most recently, but never asked about them or anything else in her life. And she'd shared almost nothing with him. The conversation when he'd revealed his suspicion that they'd met before was the only time. Considering their situation here, she would have no call to speak on such things.

'I was married.' Another shudder racked her before she could control it. 'For almost a year.' She met his gaze, praying to all the gods that she would not see pity there. His eyes were clear of any emotion, but she noticed his hands kept clenching into fists as she spoke.

'He died,' she explained before he would have to ask her. 'Four years ago.'

'Painfully?' She felt a smile threaten as his one uttered word seemed to be in her defence, years later.

'Not nearly enough for my taste.' His gaze warmed as he nodded. 'He died on a voyage with my father. I never learned the details of how it happened. I didn't care at the time or even since.' She winced then at the terrible way those words sounded, even to her.

'Many people seem to die on voyages on your father's ships.' She heard no humour in his tone.

'What do you mean?' Katla rearranged her gown and tucked her legs beneath her. She did not feel strong enough to stand on her own yet.

'Your husband. My brother nearly died on one of his ships to Constantinople and the man we believe actually killed my father did perish on it.'

He clamped his mouth shut too late, the words were out and his vow not to reveal anything to her was broken already. Nothing had happened to make him believe her trustworthy. Indeed, she could be about her father's work even now. Yet, as he watched her speak about her dead husband and her father's plan for a new marriage, he could not find it in him to believe she lied. Though this new arrangement with his aunt's commander felt damning and far too convenient to him.

The marriage would tie Thorfinn more closely to Kolga in a way he wasn't yet. Oh, they had been married a number of years, but each continued to live their own lives—his aunt, as he'd heard, rarely left the north while Thorfinn divided his time between his lands there and here. It was stranger to him that Thorfinn did not press to have her marry Eithr rather than a common soldier.

Eithr was spoiled and more child than man and not a warrior trained or experienced. When he was born weak and sickly, suggestions had been made to expose him to the gods. Kolga had refused to allow it and the man-boy sat on the throne of Brandt's father, no doubt having played some part in his downfall. Eithr, who was not known for his intelligence, was more likely a pawn in his mother's plans. Which did not excuse his cousin's role, but it did explain much.

'Why do you not just sneak away? Travel to kin…?'

'My mother's family has lived on these lands for generations, since before the Norse arrived here. Any family I have are here.' She let out a breath. 'And no one will go against my father. Or my stepmother.'

If she was lying, he could not tell. Her body still trembled in fear and her eyes were haunted. Brandt noticed the dark patches under those eyes that told him of sleepless nights.

'How do you think I can help you?' he asked, sitting down on the stool she'd vacated. 'I am the prisoner here.'

'If I help you get out of here, out of the keep and away from the village, you could take us some place safe. Some place away from my father's influence. A place where they do not know his name or fear his power.'

So many places, here in Alba, out in the western islands, even south in the land of the Saxons, would be safe for her. Any of his brothers would offer her sanctuary if he took her to them. But, if she was going to betray Brandt, she would also reveal his brothers' whereabouts if she knew them. Four good men who had struggled to find a life after all they'd had was ripped from them. And each of them had found a woman who filled their hearts and they'd settled down in new lives. Unless Brandt was successful, he understood that he would never see them again.

Nay, he could not take the chance and expose them to danger because of the warm feelings he had for this young woman. He needed far better reasons than that.

'Why should I trust you, Katla Thorfinnsdottir? You can destroy all that I have left in the world by passing on what I say to your father. Are you his spy?'

Faster than he expected, she moved, standing and crossing the space between them in two long, quick strides. The sound of her hand on his face echoed around them before the sting of the strong blow startled him. Brandt should be angry but, when she cursed, he could not stop smiling.

'You stupid, stupid man! How did you live to manhood being so…so…so…?'

Watching her expressive eyes, he could imagine steam, like that above the hot spring near his village, emerging from her ears as her anger boiled over and exploded. Brandt did not even mind the second slap, for her face filled with strength, her cheeks flushed with colour and her green eyes sparkled like the lights in the sky during the winter. She was…magnificent when she was angry.

'Stupid?' he asked, grabbing her hand before a third blow landed. She tugged her hand free and shook it—clearly it had suffered as much as his face.

'Aye. As I have said before, I could have ended your life easily many times. If I'd walked away. If I'd told my father you were too close to death. If I'd simply *wanted to*, you would be dead.' She blew out a rough breath and shook her head, walking away as she muttered more foul words. Gods above and below, he loved it when she did that! 'You are just as bad as he is. He told me to spy on you and I refused.'

He'd crossed the cell and grabbed her hand before he'd thought of doing so. Brandt pulled her to face him and then tugged her closer still.

'He asked you to spy on me?'

'What?' She shook her head, looking confused over what she'd revealed. Waving him off with her other hand, she shrugged. 'Aye, of course he did. He expects me to serve his needs.'

'And you think I am daft for my suspicions? You just admitted that your father ordered you to do so!'

He released her hand and let his arms fall to his sides, staring at her. Half of him wondered how she would explain this and the other half cared not as long as she kept talking…and cursing him under her breath. Her eyes flashed once more before she exhaled slowly.

''Twas his request—but I did not agree.' He raised an eyebrow at her choice of words. 'When he ordered me to report back anything you say about the evidence you've found or about your brothers, I realised he is desperate. And desperate men are dangerous men.'

'Are they?' he asked, lowering his voice then as her tone spoke of past experiences he could not bear to learn.

'Aye. So, I knew it was time that I come up with a plan to get my sister and myself to safety. Away from his schemes. Away from this marriage that will end in my death.'

'Katla—' Her placid acceptance of such a risk pierced his soul. He stopped and wondered how to proceed. Going back to the stool in the corner, he sat down and nodded. 'Do you have a plan on how we get out of here together? Without being seen? And one that gives us enough time to get far from Wik and Katanes before an alarm is raised?' That would stop her, he was certain of it.

'The beginnings of one.' She walked nearer to him and crossed her arms over her lovely breasts then. He tried not to notice how they moved with every deep and fast breath she took, pressing against the fabric of the Norse-style gown she wore. Oh, hell, he gave up and stared his fill. 'But I need a man who is—'

'Stupid?' He laughed when he said it, even knowing it made him appear exactly that.

'I was going to say strong,' she said. A smile broke across her face and he stared at that, enjoying the way it made her look younger and less…haunted. 'A woman alone cannot travel freely and safely and surely not in the winter countryside. So, I need a man's help in this.'

Her words surprised him, for they were laden with more meanings than she must have intended. Or mayhap only he mistook them? But underlying whatever she'd meant was the thing that he'd noticed.

A woman alone cannot travel freely.

A woman alone...

His aunt could not have carried out such a widespread plot involving men from other villages and, indeed, countries, without the help of a man. Or men. With other thoughts swirling around, he knew he could neither commit to nor deny her request for help. What else could she tell him if he let her, nay, encouraged her to plan and to talk? Brandt decided that he would say only what he needed to in order to keep her coming back here and sharing her knowledge with him—about the keep, the warriors, the stores, the walls and his aunt and her father.

'Katla, I must think on this. There is much to speak about before I can know if it would even be possible.'

Devilment filled him then and he would blame it again on the way she worried her teeth over that poor, full lower lip. He wanted to lick it and taste it when she did that. He wanted to taste her. His body responded to the sight of her and his rising desire very quickly then. To test her mettle, to see if she was serious about this or if it was a ploy for her father, he smiled, stood and moved closer to her.

'However, I did not ask you one thing, Katla. One thing we must discuss first.'

'What?' she stuttered as she lifted her face to watch his.

Her eyes stared at him, wide like an animal running from a predator. Her mouth and that inviting now plump lower lip drew him and he fought for control. He felt her breath escape from her open mouth, heated and soft against his chin. It would take no effort at all to dip the scant inches between them and kiss her as he wanted to right then. But it took control that he almost lost several times in the struggle not to touch his mouth to hers. Not to lose himself in her. Lifting his head until he could no longer feel her breath moving over his skin, he smiled.

'What do I get if I help you?'

She cursed softly at his question and his body went hard, every bit of him.

'Your freedom? To seek a new life, mayhap with your brothers?'

'Ah, but my task is not that. 'Tis to seek justice and kill those responsible for my family's destruction. Katla, I have no desire to escape from here.'

He dug his fingers into his palms to keep from reaching up and caressing her face. A loose curl begged for his fingers to touch it and Brandt began to pay heed to his breaths to regain his waning control. Another moment or two this close to her and he swore he would reach across to her.

She closed her eyes then and he could see that she struggled, too. But he doubted she fought the same needs he did. She no doubt lived in fear of them. While he…he wanted her. When she opened them and gazed at him, he could see the confusion in her eyes.

'I… I will give you whatever you desire, Brandt Sigurdsson. Whatever I have to give is yours if you will help me.'

Chapter Ten

Katla cursed in silence then, not wanting him to realise how badly she'd worded her offer. Oh, the way his gaze caught fire and the way it moved over her body, stopping along the way, told her what he thought she was offering. Worse, for a moment—just the space between taking a breath and letting it out—she did not fear that he would accept the offer she'd inadvertently made by tripping over her words.

When he lowered his face to her, standing so close that the urge to touch his naked chest and stomach and revel in his strength and male beauty threatened to overwhelm her senses, she wanted to lift her mouth to his and open for him. Her body wanted his in a way she'd not felt before. She understood that it was arousal that made her breasts feel heavy and that spread heat through her whole body. Once she had married, the women of the household spoke of such things openly with her, but she had never felt it when being pummelled and forced to submit by Trygg.

Even now her fingers itched to touch him and she fought that urge with every bit of control she could find within her. He'd not been the stupid one here. She should've seen the signs as this warrior gained back his vigour. His appetite. She should step away from him right now. Allow the cold air that blew in through cracks from the outside to cool things down. To cool her down.

Instead, her traitorous mouth lifted until it touched his.

And he kissed her.

At first, just his lips touched hers, sliding and gliding against hers until the gentle pressure made her open. When he used his tongue to dip inside, she lost her balance. And her control. In spite of warnings clanging in her head, she slid her hands along his arms and held on to his massive shoulders to keep from falling.

His tongue was hot and he chased hers until he touched it and drew it into his mouth and suckled it. Heat, inside her, from him, surged through her and she pressed against him. She felt his chuckle against her mouth and yet he did nothing else but…kiss her.

The kiss changed then, becoming something more possessive, more claiming, just more. When she could not hear her thoughts or those warnings, he lifted his mouth from hers and looked into her eyes. Katla had no idea what message was in hers, but staring at Brandt she saw desire and need, questions and a bit of confusion. She had to release her hold on him when he stepped back a pace and her body mourned the loss of his closeness and heat immediately.

What was happening to her?

Where was the terror that usually filled her at the thought of being this close to a man? At being in his power. At recognising the flare of lust and remembering the consequences of that. Brandt Sigurdsson was a bigger threat to her than she'd realised for he was her enemy and she'd not only let him close, she'd pulled him in!

'That…,' he began in a deep voice before stopping to clear his throat. 'That was my price for now, Katla.'

'A kiss? You will help me for that?' She'd thought he wanted more, that he wanted her, but…only a kiss? A feeling of insult settled on her.

He shook his head and laughed. 'Nay, not for "only a kiss".' He crossed his arms over his chest and it made him seem larger and stronger. 'That was the price of considering whether I can or should help you. We must talk about certain things before I agree or refuse.'

'Certain things?' She felt as though the ground beneath her was shifting and she could find no purchase. 'What things?' Katla admitted to herself that his kiss had thrown her into some sort of storm of feelings and fears. She inhaled and exhaled, let her shoulders relax and then looked at him. 'What details will you need?'

'Things like the pattern that the guards use to protect the walls. Is there a postern or other hidden gate we can use to get out of the walls? When are the fewest people within the keep? When are the most? How many guards or warriors in the village and how many on the roads, north, west and south? And more. Those kinds of details will determine if we could successfully escape.' He lifted his chin. 'I will not undertake a task like this if it ends in my death without facing the King to demand justice.'

'So, you would take us and return?'

'Aye. I told you I will not be persuaded to abandon my search for justice.' He let out a breath. ''Tis the reason I live, in spite of your father's efforts.'

'Daft man,' she whispered.

'Senseless woman,' he muttered back.

'You could build a new life, if not with your brothers, then in another place. A man like you...' She paused at his uplifted brow. 'An experienced warrior like you would be of value to any noble or landowner, Brandt.'

'Until the honour debt I owe my father and my wife and the others is fulfilled, I can have no other life. No matter—' He stopped and his face hardened as she watched. 'No matter the cost, Katla. No matter the cost.'

When he stared at her with those last words, she shivered at the warning at the heart of them. Would he betray her plan to save his own? Was her trust misplaced yet again? Nay, somehow she knew she could have faith in him.

'If you want to go through with this plan of yours, come back when you can. We can speak more and see how foolhardy or stupid we both might be to consider it at all.'

She felt the dismissal more keenly as he walked

around her to the pallet and waited for her to leave. As she watched him, her body still throbbed with an awareness that was foreign to her. Katla wanted to kiss him or hit him all in the same moment and to laugh, remembering his earlier words about how it might feel good to do something like that. Instead, she gathered her wits about her—the ones that had scattered on her arrival here this night—and made her way back out of the cell and to her chamber.

Exhausted from long hours of overseeing the household, Katla should have fallen to sleep quickly, but some time later she lay still awake in her bed. Her body was not ready to sleep. Her thoughts spun around and tangled. As she shifted around, trying to find comfort, she realised how difficult and dangerous this endeavour would be. And, she had no way of knowing if they would succeed or not.

Well, if she could not sleep, she would try to sort through her plan of escape. Brandt was correct—there were so many elements of this that would have to be prepared well. From timing to what they took with them. From the direction they would take to how they would get out of the keep and castle. The most difficult matter for Katla, after she allowed herself to believe Brandt would help her and not reveal her plans to anyone, was to come up with the best way to approach her sister about this.

She'd shielded Gemma from as much as she could over the years. Katla had twisted the truth and plainly lied in an attempt to keep the worst of things away from her younger, innocent sister. She would have to convince Gemma to leave with her. How would she do that? How could she reveal her own shame and weakness to the one person who looked up to her?

She shook her head at that. She would deal with it when the time came. In revealing the matter too soon, she could jeopardise all of them. Katla's only regret would be in leaving her aunt behind. The older woman had lived in this household and on these lands for decades, lands that had been passed down in her mother's family until the Norse arrived on their shores and took it from them. Alpia had many kith and kin here and would be safer here than fleeing in the late winter along roads that would be difficult and sometimes unpassable.

When the day dawned bright and sunny, Katla had not fallen asleep and, even if she could have remained abed for a little longer, she pushed off the furs and blankets and dressed for the day. Mayhap she could take advantage of the turn in the weather and take her sister to the village when she went to check on the miller's wife. It would give her a chance to begin her plan or to at least prepare her sister for the truths she would learn if Katla somehow left without her.

Katla might, if this plan did not work, leave to go north when forced to, but she would not do it willingly and not without a way to protect her sister from facing the same fate as she did. As she left after her maid braided and tied up her unruly hair, Katla offered prayers to Freya and even to Frigga for guidance and protection as she went about her day. And she looked for an opportunity to speak with Gemma away from the listening ears and watching eyes of those who would report back to their father.

Brandt did not need to be roused from sleep that morning—he had never fallen asleep. How could a man when he'd been tempted almost to madness? Although the exhaustion of fighting to control every impulse and need in him to take her, take what she clearly offered, should have made sleep easy, it did not.

He remembered the exact moment when the expression in her eyes and the way she stared at his mouth warned him. She had moved closer and closer until he could feel her breath on his face. Then, her mouth, by the gods! Her mouth touched his and he nearly lost his senses. Warm. Welcoming. In no longer than a single moment, everything he wanted to do to and with her flashed through his mind and his body readied itself for all of it. When she slid her hands along his arms and grabbed on to his shoulders to steady herself, Brandt thought he would explode into a ravening beast.

Only the inexperience and innocence of her kiss stopped him.

For, married or not, bedded or not, Katla Thorfinnsdottir did not know how to kiss. What kind of man does not take the time to teach his wife and to learn her ways? That had stopped him short. From her words and his observations, he knew what kind of man she'd been married to and the answer to his question. When he'd finally paused in his efforts to possess her mouth and had lifted his head, he'd seen something in her gaze that had terrified him: surrender.

He was not the man to accept such surrender. Not from her. Not here. Not in this place or time. For that would mean stopping to accept her. To take her into his life and into his...

Nay. He could not be that man, so he'd stepped back away from her, from her offer, from...her. He'd recognised the hurt in her gaze then, but he would not let that stop him. Better to keep things separate and, if he did decide he could help her get away from her father, even to one of his brothers, his plan to prove his father had been betrayed was not something he could walk away from.

So, when they led him out into the yard to work, Brandt used it to release the pent-up need and want she'd caused with that damn kiss. And with the way she stared at him, offering herself in trade without truly understanding what the hell she was doing. And, damn it, with the way she sighed into his mouth and stroked his arms and pressed against his body.

He groaned aloud then, gaining the attention of the guards and those closest in the yard carrying out their own tasks. He shrugged at the guard closest, rolled his shoulders as if they hurt and continued on. Soon, they ignored him while going about their own duties while the sun warmed the late winter day.

The last days had been one storm after another, so much of the labour he did was inside one building or another. Thorfinn's home was not like northern longhouses, with their thatched roofs and wooden structures. Buildings like that would never withstand the winds and storms that battered the coast here. So this stone house, with its stone wall surrounding it, stood a better chance than any others might.

He thought of Maerr for the first time in a long while and knew that the inlet on which it sat protected it from the worst of the weather. Not being on the coast allowed the harbour to be spared the heaviest storms and winds. Set in the gentle slopes of the mountains that began nearby, Maerr was in a perfect place. He wondered if Old Olaf yet built boats at the water's edge or if his son had mastered the skills of his father. And did the fields above the village yield good crops?

Brandt stared off for a moment, thinking of how much it must have changed in the time since he'd last been home. They'd had to flee not long after the massacre when the first accusations were made about his father. They had hidden Alarr so he could recover and then tried to reclaim what should have been theirs, but it was too late. Too many lies told, too many machinations accomplished that robbed them of their birthright.

Gods, how he missed all of them and that place!

The guard shoved him then and Brandt turned back to his work. It was better not to think of the people and things they'd lost. He was a warrior, experienced and good at killing, but that did not mean he was a fool who overestimated his chances at accomplishing what he set out to do here. Not when the initial challenge had gone as it did and he'd been a prisoner for this long. If he could kill Thorfinn before the King, at least the stain of dishonour would be removed.

* * *

A short while later, they took him through the gate to work on the other side of the wall, repairing damage from the storm. Brandt realised he had an opportunity to watch the guards as he worked and see their patterns and scheduled movements. He had not yet decided whether her plan was ambitious or foolhardy, but he would take advantage of the time out of his prisoner cell and collect his own information.

He busied himself counting guards while he worked, pausing now and then to watch as they moved from place to place atop the walls and the gates. With the unusual break in the winter storms, many of those from the village moved about the area, coming to the keep and staring at him as they did. Word had spread about his identity because he heard the furtive whispers of his name as they passed. Brandt ignored them for the most part, paying heed only to those he thought important...or dangerous. Only when a woman answered someone hailing her did he pause in his work.

'My lady! My lady!' a woman called across the road. 'Did you see the babe?'

'Aye, we have just visited her,' Katla called out. 'The gods have blessed your sister with a healthy babe.'

He could not help himself then—he turned to see her. Her voice was so full of joy and so different from how she spoke to him in those dark hours of night and day in his prison. Either she was cursing him for his stupidity or fighting for him to survive or offering herself in an impossible bargain, though never just speaking. Before he turned to look at her, Brandt realised he'd never seen her in the light of day. He had some fleeting memory of meeting the gaze of a woman the day he arrived here in the midst of the challenge with Thorfinn, but could not be certain if it had been her or not.

If he had thought her magnificent in the throes of anger, the flush after their passionate kiss or in the intense times when she had treated his wounds and saved his life, this Katla, standing in the light of a bright midday sun, would be his favourite sight of her. The gleam of the light reflecting off her blonde curls nearly blinded him. As she moved, the sun touched her face, her skin, her smile, and made her appear like a goddess. Though she wore a plain, serviceable gown under her heavy cloak, no one could ever mistake her for a common villager. Her gentle manners drew others who'd been nearby and she spoke to each one, asking them questions and drawing the girl at her side into the exchanges.

Then she laughed aloud, and Brandt smiled at the sound of it once more. But when she glanced over and met his gaze, he thought his heart had stopped beating. Only a moment passed before he gathered his wits about him and turned away, else the guards would remind him of his work. When he bent down to pick up another rock to move it from the road, he chanced another look over at her.

The gods must have directed his attention back, for a wagon bound for the castle's gate hit a deep, icy rut in the road and overturned just behind Katla. Dangerous shards of wood and a wheel careened towards her and her sister and, without thinking, he ran across the road. If his guards shouted warnings, he heard them not. If others moved to help, he did not see them. In that blink of an eye all he could see was her. And the danger headed her way.

He shoved the younger woman out of the way and used his body to shield Katla from the onslaught of debris, wrapping himself around her and rolling into the snowbank at the side of the road. Silence ruled for a scant time and then the uproar began around the area. But he did not release her immediately, he only stared at her until she drew in a breath and opened her eyes.

'Are you well, Katla?' he whispered, searching her face for any sign of injury.

'You saved me,' she said on a breath. 'I…'

'I have to save you a few more times to catch up to the number of times you have saved me.' He glanced over his shoulder at the approaching guards. 'Just tell me you are not injured.'

A shake of her head was all he got before the guards dragged him away. He shoved free and moved back to where he'd been working on his own, then, and watched as workers from within the yard poured out to help gather up the goods and supplies that had been thrown out of the wagon. Thorfinn strode out, his commander at his side, to see the damage.

'Take him within!' Alfaran yelled. 'Now!'

Brandt guessed the commander thought he would try to escape in the mayhem that still ebbed and flowed around the scene of the accident. When Thorfinn walked towards him, Brandt thought about attacking him then and ending it, one way or another. It would

take them all by surprise. It might even kill the Jarl who
Brandt held responsible for the plot against his family.
But then Katla walked behind her father towards him
and he knew he could not. He let out a breath as the
guards grabbed his arms and held him.

'You saved my daughters,' Thorfinn said, searching Brandt's face as though he would find some answer there. 'Did you think I would release you for such
an act?'

Brandt laughed then—he had not even considered
something like that. He had simply acted when Katla
was in danger.

'Do not forget, Thorfinn the Betrayer, I do not seek
release. I will remain here until I get the truth and reclaim my father's honour before the King.' Brandt's
words were loud enough that many heard them.

Thorfinn moved like the warrior he was then, slam-
ming his fist into Brandt's face. When he could shake
the pain off, Brandt recovered his footing and stood
tall. It would take more than one punch to lay him low,
even in his weakened state. The guards tightened their
grips on him as Thorfinn moved closer and Brandt prepared for another blow. It never came.

Brandt noticed Katla's pale face and wide eyes
then. Her hands clenched into fists and released as if
she wanted to punch someone. He smiled at her then,
knowing that he would teach her to do that before he
left her. She would, he thought, find some power and
some release in being able to fight back. That was
mayhap the biggest difference, among many, between
her and Ingrid—Katla was a warrior while Ingrid had

not been. Oh, Katla spent much of her time caring and healing others, but the soul within her was that of a warrior. Ingrid had been a gentle creature at heart.

Thorfinn's anger disappeared then and he nodded to the guards to take him as Alfaran had ordered them. After a few paces, Thorfinn called out once more to the guards.

'Double his daily portions for saving my daughters' lives.'

If anyone else thought that this order was strange, they gave no indication by word or deed. A man who had worked for several years to wipe Brandt's family out of existence, yet now he gave him more food... Food that would serve to keep him alive and well. Food that would make him strong, strong enough to fight...

He truly needed to understand more about this man. At times, his actions seemed to say he wanted Brandt alive and well. Other times, well...as he thought on it, Brandt realised that following the initial fight and Thorfinn's discovery of his condition after being left for dead by Alfaran, Thorfinn had done nothing to endanger him. As he walked back to the cell, the surprise of the realisation struck him. If the man had wanted Brandt dead, he would be dead. Not only that, unless he had specifically wanted him alive, he would be dead, either through the actions of his men or the inactions of his jailors.

Brandt shook his head over all that he still did not understand.

Somehow, more than before, he wanted to. Nothing seemed right in this. Was it possible that the knowledge he carried was not the truth? Or mayhap not the whole of it? Thorfinn's behaviour made no sense and he needed to know why.

The one person who could help him understand was the one person who needed his help. And the person whose life *he'd* just saved.

And, he suspected, the same person who would be sneaking down here in the middle of the night. She needed help. He needed answers. A perfect arrangement.

The only thing that worried him was that same person—Katla Thorfinnsdottir. She was far more dangerous than anyone here believed. They saw the healer, the caregiver, the dutiful daughter serving her father.

He saw the fierce fighter, the beautiful angel of mercy and the warrior goddess who would protect those she loved. He saw the woman who wanted to throw off her past and embrace a new life.

Worse, he saw a woman he could share a life with. A woman he would be pleased to have at his side, in good and in bad.

All the time he'd thought that the danger to him was from Thorfinn or his men. He'd never considered that a woman would be the weakest part of his plan... or the most powerful.

Gods above and below, but he was the fool here! As the hours moved at a painfully slow pace, Brandt resolved not to be caught in his own game. Find out what he needed to be ready for the journey north. Avoid any entanglements. Resist the temptation of a certain woman.

* * *

When the door opened late that night, he thought he heard Loki the Trickster laugh and wondered if he'd been abandoned by the other gods.

Chapter Eleven

He'd fallen asleep while waiting for her to arrive that night. The huge bowl of stew brought to him and the skin of ale filled his belly, making it easier to fall into sleep's grasp. So, he missed the sound of her approach and only woke when the key clinked in the door. Brandt rubbed his eyes and face and sat up on the pallet as she entered.

'Do you ever rest?' he asked as she closed the door and approached.

The ever-present basket hung on her arm and the lantern's light revealed her exhaustion. Gone was the bright laughing face and flashing eyes of earlier today. Her hair was gathered in its practical arrangement to keep it out of her face when she worked.

'I do.' The wide and noisy yawn that followed belied her words. 'Well, I try to.' Shrugging, she pulled the stool over and sat nearer to him.

'Then I will not keep you here for too long this

night, if you promise to seek out your bed when we are finished.'

''Tis not that I don't seek my rest,' she said. 'The dreams or fretting over what is to come keep me awake most nights.' Had she realised she'd admitted something so private to a man who was her enemy? A man who should be looking for weaknesses to exploit? So the words he spoke as that man, as that enemy and that man, shocked even him.

'I have suffered those kinds of dreams, too.'

Her gaze softened then, seeming less haunted and more concerned now. Why had he revealed such a thing to her?

'With all the loss you have suffered, I am not surprised, Brandt. So much grief. So much pain.'

She was trying to comfort him.

She was trying to comfort *him*.

His ability to approach her and their situation in a practical manner was fading quickly with every incursion under his own defences she made like this. Applying her healing skills at her father's orders was one thing—this though, this was a completely different and more dangerous one. He stood there and walked to the door, on the pretence of checking the corridor beyond it.

'I was able to count the guards on the wall earlier,' he said, pushing the topic under discussion as far away from its current focus as he could. 'Does that number change at night? Fewer? More?'

'Were you injured by the debris, Brandt?' Gods

damn! But her voice was closer now. 'I brought my supplies to tend to you.'

He did not turn around. He shook his head and tried to ignore the softness of her voice. He'd almost succeeded when she touched his shoulder. Her finger traced his skin and he could not breathe.

'You are bleeding here,' she said. 'And here, as well.'

He turned and found her as close as he'd suspected she was. Her hand was still in the space between them, but she dropped it and smiled at him.

'I find I must thank you for saving me this day,' she said in a voice barely louder than a whisper. 'For a moment, I thought it might have been easier if you had not.'

Brandt blinked several times at her disclosure. Had her words not mirrored his own thoughts when he'd first roused from sickness? If Thorfinn had killed him then, clean and simple, leaving him no other difficult choices to make, no more battles to fight, no more...

'But then, it would leave Gemma behind without a word and without protection. And I could not willingly do that.' Tears shone in those green eyes and she glanced away for a moment. 'Not willingly.' Meeting his gaze now, the tears were gone and replaced with resolve. 'Do you wish me to tend to those while we speak about guards and walls?'

Once more the shield maiden rose within her and she brought her attention to this plan of hers. He shrugged and shook his head.

'Nay, I am well,' he said. He waved his hand back at the stool and waited for her to sit. 'I did not notice any guards on the road into the village when I arrived. Does Alfaran not post them at such places?'

''Tis usual to have at least one on each approach—from the north and the south. Some days, he sends out patrols rather than standing guards.'

'So, we can expect to run into one guard or a patrol, then?' he asked. Though he meant it in jest, she nodded. 'Are they in position in the night as well the day?'

Katla shook her head then and smiled. Like a cat ready to lick its whiskers. 'They usually go out just before sunset and return by nightfall.'

'So, any escape you plan must be after dark.'

'Any escape I plan?'

'I have not yet agreed to this, Katla. I need to know more.'

Brandt had already decided he would help her. He could see her and the girl to safety and return here or to the north to make his case before the King or the Althing, the yearly gathering where disputes were heard and judged. And if it would tweak Thorfinn's nose for him to do it, all the better.

He needed more details about the way things worked here or what possible dangers they would face. Other than the escape itself. Or getting out of the keep. Or the yard. And the village. And Katanes and so on. The more he understood, the more he could plan.

They spoke for a while about the other places that guards would be and how many were in the hall or the yard on any given day. When a yawn broke free from her, Brandt shook his head.

'You must go.'

'There is more you must know. To make your decision,' she protested. Another yawn weakened her argument.

'We have weeks to prepare for this,' he said, standing before her. 'Go. Rest. The morn breaks too soon.' He saw the moment she surrendered to the weariness. Katla walked to the door and turned to face him before opening it.

'Before I go,' she said. She shifted her basket up on her arm and retrieved the key from where she kept it inside her sleeve. 'My father did send me to spy on you. You knew that.' He nodded. 'I am not his spy, Brandt. On my sister's life, I swear it.' She did not place value on her own life. A sadness pierced him then as he understood that.

'I would not be speaking to you about any of this if I thought you were, Katla.'

As he said the words, he knew they were the truth. He might need her for the knowledge she would share with him, but he did not believe she would betray him in this. Not now. Not since…she'd thanked him for saving her life. Something had shifted within him this day and he would not be able to turn it back.

'My father, well, my father expects me to tell him what you say. About him and my stepmother. About your brothers. About the evidence you have.'

He froze at the mention of his brothers and their proof. Even speaking of them was a threat and a bigger one when he was mulling over how trustworthy she was on that matter. If she'd admitted her father's demands and sworn on her sister's life, could he trust her now? Katla lifted her hand to reach out to him and stopped when she saw the hesitation in him. He stepped—nay, leaned back ever so slightly, yet enough for her to notice.

'Just give me something I can tell him. If he changes his mind, he will assign guards in this corridor and every place you—and I—are. My plan fails. You will die because you will not gain what you need most. So, Brandt, I beg you, tell me something.'

Her voice shook. She was bone-weary and ready to fall, even he could see that in the shadows of night.

'My father will summon me in the morn and ask me for this and if I have nothing with which to placate him, everything will fail.' Katla shivered then and her voice was so soft he could hardly hear her. But he did. 'And I, we, cannot fail in this.'

He could not doubt her need. What could he share that would not endanger his brothers? He spoke softly, too, as he offered her something she could use.

'After Alarr healed, the five of us escaped from the north that is under King Harald's control and went our separate ways. We scattered to the western isles, Éireann, Alba and even to the lands of the Picti and the Saxons.' He lifted his eyes and met her gaze. 'Is that enough to keep your father's suspicions allayed?'

'Aye.' She nodded and when he thought she would leave, she paused. Without facing him, she whispered. 'Truly, I thank you for saving me this day. I have no fear of dying, but I fear for my sister if I die too soon.'

Her words gutted him as surely as if she'd taken a knife and slashed his belly wide open. The strange thing was that rather than pitying her because of her words, her certainty imbued them with courage. She was the shield maiden once more even if she carried no sword or axe. Then she was gone—the key turned quickly in the door and her footsteps echoing behind her—before he could utter a word.

Which was a good thing, for Brandt could not find words to say.

The gods blessed them with another cold, clear day on the morrow and Katla asked Gemma and their aunt to join her in a walk once more. Alpia had not left the keep the day before, claiming her old bones ached too much, but Katla did not allow her that excuse this time. After speaking to her father and giving him the details that Brandt had provided, the three made their way across the icy yard and out the gate to the road. She had no definite destination in mind, it was more that she wanted to assess her aunt's abilities to walk and move about on the rugged and uneven road and land.

Though she had not discussed it with Brandt, she now hoped to take her aunt with them when they escaped. At first, Katla suspected that her aunt's life-long connections might hold her here in spite of any appeal on Katla's part when they escaped. Alpia had been her stalwart companion through all the challenges and changes that life had thrown at her, especially over the last five years.

Once again, they were greeted warmly by the villagers who scurried out of the cottages into the sun, for however long it would last. It was not long before Gemma saw some of the girls of her age and went off with them. Katla waved Aife off to follow along with the girls. Soon, she and Alpia reached the end of the village on the road south without catching sight of Brandt working or any guards at their positions. She pointed to a large rock just off the path where Alpia could rest.

'You did well, Aunt,' Katla said. 'After all your complaints about this infirmity or that ache or pain, I thought I was going to have to leave you behind at the gates.' Katla kept watch as her aunt made her way to the rock and sat on it. Alpia did not wince or walk with a limp. And she seemed at ease when she sat on the flat surface or as she shifted around to find a comfortable position.

'You are staring, Niece,' Alpia said. She laughed then as she moved away from the edge to the centre. 'Come. Sit. 'Tis warmed from the sun, but it won't last.'

Katla sat next to her aunt and enjoyed the heat of the rock beneath them. They sat in companionable silence for a short time before her aunt spoke.

'The prisoner seems recovered.'

'Aye. Other than the new scrapes and cuts from the cart overturning yesterday, aye, he seems well.'

'And did you tend to those in the middle of the night?'

Katla let out a sigh. ''Twas the least I could do for him, Aunt. When a man saves your life…'

'I heard so many versions of the story before you even returned to the hall! So many people saw it happen. How he ran to save you when he saw the cart crash. How he wrapped himself around you and threw you both to the ground away from the danger. How he flung Gemma aside even while running to you.'

All Katla could do was turn and stare at her aunt's words. No one had spoken a word to her after the incident. No one. Her father had not even asked after her later at supper. Even Aife, who'd been following along, but had been farther from the accident and not endangered by it, had said nothing about it as she helped Katla ready for bed. Yet, clearly, others had much to say and say them to her aunt they did.

'Such a strong, brave man,' her aunt said on a sigh of her own.

'Prisoner, Aunt Alpia. He is a prisoner. Of my father.'

'Oh, even at his weakest or worst, Brandt Sigurdsson is a strong man.'

'What point are you trying to make here? Aye, Brandt Sigurdsson is a strong man. Brave to have tried to rescue me. Fine. So? He is still Father's prisoner and will die when they go north to the King.' Katla slid off the now cooling rock to stand before her aunt. 'He will die and I will…face my fate worse than death,' she spat out the words as the anger within her rose.

'And all because my father married that witch from Maerr. All because she was powerful enough or strong enough or evil enough to pull him under her control.' The fury poured out of her now, safe somehow when spoken to her aunt. 'If he had never met her, I would not be in this situation. If he would refuse her, I would be safe.'

Katla did not realise she was pacing until her aunt spoke her name. She turned to face the woman who'd been like a mother to her in the years since her mother, and Alpia's sister, had died. She'd interceded with her father. She'd bandaged the bruises and damage after he took his rage out on Katla. She'd helped protect Gemma from seeing the worst.

'Why? If I only understood why?' The question came out as a cry and Katla hated the weak sound of it. 'Something changed when he met her. He'd been a harsh, demanding father all my life, but after she entered our lives, he became what is he now—the ever-angry man who seems to do whatever she says.'

'Did you ask him about her?' Katla shook her head. 'What about this marriage to her commander?' Katla nodded then and Alpia slid to her feet and stood next to her. Her eyes were filled with concern and looked so much like her mother's that Katla had to look away for a moment to regain her control.

'Aye. He said there is much I do not know and cannot know. And he said he was sorry.' The way her aunt's eyes widened then told Katla that the older woman was just as surprised at that action as Katla had been.

'He has never apologised for anything he's done,' her aunt said, a bitter undertone flowing through her words making it sound more like an accusation.

Alpia had known her father longer than she had, had seen him in his younger years when he was married to her sister and through the dark days of Modwenna's illness and passing. In all these years, Katla had never asked her aunt about any of it. Alpia resisted any efforts to speak of those days or about her mother and father's marriage. Katla had accepted it was painful for her and had never pressed her.

But what did she know? Could she help Katla to understand it all? And could their knowledge together help Brandt convince the King that her father and step-mother were in league to destroy the sons and family of Sigurd?

'What is the matter, Katla? Your face has lost all its colour.'

The thought of helping Brandt should have repulsed her. She should be horrified by the possibility of aiding an enemy and yet Katla knew she would. If her father was innocent, if her stepmother was not behind these gruesome acts, then they could prove it, too.

She looked at her aunt. Whether it was that new self-awareness or the building desperation within her, Katla understood her aunt knew much, much more than she'd ever spoken of.

'Tell me the truth, Aunt Alpia. Tell me why and how my father is in the middle of this plot against Sigurd's sons and why I am dragged into the middle of it.'

'Come to my chamber after everyone is asleep and I will tell you what I know.'

Now, sadness filled the old woman's gaze and, for a moment, dread filled Katla's heart at what truths her aunt would reveal. For once spoken of, those secrets could never be ignored again.

No matter that the winds were strong, Katla sought out her refuge in the middle of the night. Standing against the wall and facing the sea, she tried to organise her thoughts and her feelings about the truths her aunt had told her. With her eyes closed, she sifted through all the words she'd heard to the ones that nearly took her to her knees.

Thorfinn Bjornsson was not her father.

He'd raised her and had taken care of her and her sister, her half-sister, since her birth and yet another man had fathered her. It made no sense. It was not believable. And yet it did and was. The fact explained so much of the last five or six years, but it also created more questions for her. Questions she could not ask him without exposing her newfound knowledge.

The one thing her aunt could not confirm was how he'd learned the truth. In looking back at how and when his behaviour towards her had changed, Katla could point to one reason and one thing—Kolga Olafsdottir and her marriage to her fath—to Thorfinn.

She brushed away the tears that burned her eyes. The winds were to blame for those, she was certain. Katla stepped out of the protection of the wall and let the breezes buffet her. Her hair tore free from the ties that held it in a braid and blew out behind her. Shaking it free, she allowed the winds to soothe her frayed emotions and thought on what she should do.

Alpia swore she did not know the name of the man who'd fathered Katla. Something in her words made Katla believe her aunt lied about that and she was suspicious about the reasons why her aunt would tell her this now.

To Katla though, Alpia's words had almost been an

absolution, given to free Katla from the limits of kin-ship and obedience. But, since Thorfinn had claimed her as his daughter, even telling the truth now would not free her from his dominion. She lived within his household on lands he claimed by right of marriage and in Katla's name as eldest daughter of Modwenna.

That claim could be nullified by Katla's true parentage, but words in a decades-old marriage contract would never hold up to the power of a Norse jarl and his warriors intent on stealing her inheritance. In some ways, she was more adrift now knowing the truth than she'd been when she lived unaware of it.

The only thing that did not change in her life was her sister. No matter that they did not share a father, her vow to protect Gemma still fired her resolve to escape.

Katla reached up and gathered her hair in her hands, twisting it until she could tuck it inside her cloak to control it once more. With a nod at the guard nearest to her, she made her way back inside. Standing in the freezing winds would not sort things out. Nor would trying to understand the change in her...in Thorfinn. Learning the truth did not make it easy to think of him as anything but her father. That would take time.

She untied her cloak and tossed it over her arm as she entered the keep. Walking through the hall to reach her chamber, Katla did not have to ponder on what had changed him or *who*.

The answer to both was his marriage to Kolga Olaf-sdottir.

The bigger question that she needed to understand was why. Her father had not needed to marry, unless he still wished for a son. And marriage to Kolga made that impossible due to her age.

Why had Kolga wreaked such havoc in their family? The answer to that might solve the riddle of so many other puzzles that seemed to connect through her—Kolga's marriage to Thorfinn, the change in his behaviour towards Katla and even, if Brandt was correct in his accusations, the killing of Brandt's father and his wife and other kin in that terrible massacre.

Had Thorfinn been a part of that as Brandt charged? Had he planned out such a thing to claim the throne of the small kingdom of Maerr? If he had, why? He was not in the north or even on his own lands much at all, seeking these lands in the south much more often.

Almost as if he was avoiding his wife. As if he did not wish to be with her. As if his oath to the King to stand by Eithr was a seasonal one that depended on the weather.

Katla hung her cloak on a peg by the door of her chamber and once again sent Aife off to her own bed. She wished to be alone and figure out the parts of this whole sad story that did not fit or work. Barely had she laid her head on her bed when she laughed at the strange thought that plagued her most...

What would Brandt's reaction be on discovering she was not Thorfinn's daughter after all?

Chapter Twelve

She did not return for three days. Well, three nights.

Brandt found that he did not sleep deeply, waiting for the sound of her approach. When it did not come, he was awake worrying over whether she was ill or not. Whether the exhaustion he saw worsening in her eyes had taken her down. Whether her father had beaten her. And then on to one after another dire possibilities that kept her from his cell.

The weather eased those few days, so he was kept outside working. Even so, he tried to see her each time he walked through the keep, the hall and even the yard. And did not.

It was almost as if she'd disappeared from Wik Castle.

Then, earlier than her usual custom on that third night, he heard the soft footsteps coming down the corridor towards him and he stood at the door and waited for her. The sight of a younger version of Katla standing before him with wide eyes and an open mouth surprised him into silence. Then, the girl's gaze narrowed at him and she lifted her chin just as Katla did when puzzled. Ah, this was Gemma, the sister.

He'd seen her just before the cart accident, but his sight had been so firmly on her sister that Brandt could not swear whether they shared features or not. Now, though, as she stood outside his door, lantern in hand and anger on her face, he could see the strong resemblance. The funny thing was that she wore the same kind of mutinous expression now that Danr wore when his wishes were thwarted.

'Lady,' he said, nodding to her. 'What brings you here?'

Her gaze narrowed even more before she spoke.

'What have you done to my sister?' she asked.

'Is she harmed?' he asked back. 'Is she injured?' He gripped the opening in the door. 'Where is she?'

The girl crossed her arms over the finely made gown she wore and shook her head. Her lower lip pushed forward and stubbornness covered her face.

'She is in her chamber,' she said. 'But ever since you came here, something has been wrong. She is not herself. She…is different somehow.' She tossed her head and her long, blonde curls flowed around her. 'Did you hurt her? I had heard that you struck her.'

Those green eyes so like Katla's narrowed again, waiting for him to answer. And Brandt had the unmistakable feeling that whatever reply he made would be the wrong one. He released his grasp of the opening and dropped his arms. Because he'd stepped back, it forced her to move closer and lift up on her toes to see in.

'I accidentally—'

'Ha! I knew it!' She pointed a finger at him. 'I heard—'

'When I was delirious from fever, I pulled on her arm.' He let out a breath. 'That is all,' he whispered, now feeling the need to explain his actions. 'I do not hurt women,' he said, narrowing his own gaze and adding a sneer for good measure. 'Or children.'

He let his gaze move over her from head to toe and back up again to make his point. Brandt felt as if he was arguing with a younger Danr again. And he'd rarely won those battles as he recalled.

'I am not a child.'

'Well, you are disobeying as a child does.'

The sound of Katla's voice surprised them both. Brandt stepped back a bit so she could enter if she wished. Gemma jumped back and waited for her sister to reach them.

'Gemma, this is no place for you. Go, seek your chamber. Aife is waiting for you.'

'Katla, he—'

'Your chamber. Now.' Katla's tone said she would allow no disobedience from her sister. 'You have been told to avoid him. If Father finds out you've been down here, he will be displeased. With both of us.'

From where he stood, he could see the colour drain from the girl's face at the mention of Thorfinn. She glanced from her sister to him and back to Katla before she huffed out an angry, frustrated breath and walked quickly away. Katla stood watching and did not turn to him until the door at the end of the corridor closed. The only thing that surprised him then was that Gemma had not slammed it as Danr would have done when he was that angry.

For a moment, he thought Katla was angry with him, for when she looked at him, her face was like stone. Then, she shook her head and smiled.

'I have only one younger sibling to deal with. You had four?' she asked.

'Aye. They would plot against me all together,' he explained. 'And the twins were dangerous when they set their minds to it.' He laughed then, remembering some of the exploits of the five sons of Sigurd when they were younger. 'I did not stand a chance.'

'How did you deal with it?' she asked, looking at him, but not moving to open the door. 'Four to your one?'

'I grew bigger years before they did. Size matters, it seems.'

'I fear that does not work the same for girls as it does for boys.' She shook her head once more. 'You ate supper? You are well?'

'Aye. Your father's orders to feed me more have stood and my belly is full.' He touched his stomach then. Something was wrong with her. He could not pick out what it was and he did not know if he and Gemma were thinking of the same thing, but Katla was not the same. 'Are you well, Katla?'

'Aye. I must go now and see to Gemma.'

'Will you return later when everything is settled?'

'Nay. Not this night.' He watched her as she avoided his gaze then.

'Katla? What is wrong?' Brandt moved up to the door and watched as she stepped away. Evading. Avoiding.

'Will you help me with my plan? Brandt, I must know your answer now.'

He'd thought to delay his agreement until he learned more about her father and Kolga, but one glance at the fear in her eyes now and he knew his original plan had changed and he would not deny her the help she needed. He did not examine his reasons too closely for he suspected he would find time enough in the coming nights and days to do that.

'Aye, Katla. I will help you and your sister escape.'

'We will speak soon then,' she whispered.

And then she was gone, almost as fast as her sister had disappeared, leaving Brandt to wonder over this change. He'd seen no sign of injury or illness. No new bruises marred her delicate features. She did not favour one arm or leg. Had the worry over his help or possible refusal overwhelmed her?

But, by the gods, he knew something was wrong.

It was three more days and three long nights before she visited him.

He did not rise when she entered this time. Instead he waited as she came in and sat on the stool before even sitting upright. After the strange mood that seemed in control of her the last time she'd been here, he thought it would be better to let her lead the conversation. At least, to open it. When she held out a small jug to him, he reached for it.

'This is more potent than the ale you have been drinking these last weeks. Have a care or your head will feel worse than with one of my potions.'

He pulled out the stopper, lifted it to his nose and sniffed. Gods, it smelled strong! 'Mead?'

'Aye. A good batch by the brewer. I thought you might like some.'

'My thanks,' he said, nodding at her.

Lifting the jug, he tilted it and took a taste. It was strong and heady, sweet under the burn as it covered his tongue. He drank down another mouthful before holding it out to her. She took it and drank before handing it back. Brandt put the jug down next to the pallet.

'Did Gemma get in trouble for coming here?' he asked. Her sister might be a safe subject to discuss while he sorted out what was not.

'Nay. She was not seen here or leaving. I have warned her to stay away, but her curiosity is strong.'

'That is not necessarily a bad thing, Katla.'

'You are right. Not necessarily. But... Father frowns on her explorations and I have tried to temper her behaviour—'

'But she is young and inquisitive and cannot be stopped?'

She smiled then, the first genuine one he'd seen in days, and her face lit up as she spoke of her sister. Listening to her now, he understood her fierce loyalty and her need to protect the younger sibling from the harshness of life. Yet he wanted to caution her that she could not control all that would come her sister's way, and nor should she. For now, he just watched as she told him of her sister's innate humour and intelligence and skill with needle and thread. And how she would be the perfect commander one day for she enjoyed ordering people around so much.

He could believe that after seeing the way Gemma handled herself here just days before. Not many girls her age would brave the dungeon to see a prisoner, whether curious or not, or face down a man who could kill her barehanded with little effort. Gemma Thorfinnsdottir had been furious, not afraid. Her demand to know if he'd harmed her sister surprised him.

'Her curiosity may help when we leave.' Katla brought them back to their plan. 'She might consider it all one big adventure.'

'And when she tires of the cold and snow on the roads as we cross Alba? What do we do then?'

'Gag her, tie her to a horse and go on?' she said.

He laughed then, having threatened at least one of his brothers with a similar fate for his constant bickering and whining on a journey they took one summer long ago.

'I would suggest that, but she already thinks me cruel.' She nodded and he watched that guarded expression enter and temper her bright eyes as she glanced away. 'Tell me what vexes you, Katla? Other than facing all the challenges you face and our nigh-on impossible plan to escape from Wik and your father?'

The shake of her head was so slight he would have

missed it had he not been watching her so closely just at that moment. So, something was wrong.

'Do you still wish to proceed?' The nod was more vigorous. 'Let us talk about something else, then?' She faced him. When he was about to suggest a topic, she spoke first.

'Tell me of your aunt.'

'Kolga? Your stepmother?'

'Aye. Tell me of her before she married Thorfinn.'

Brandt reached out and retrieved the jug before answering her. He'd never liked his mother's older sister, but now that they had proof she was behind the plot, he'd come to hate her more and more with each disclosure of her guilt. He took a mouthful of the mead and held it out to Katla. 'What do you want to know?'

'My father…changed when he married her. I wish to understand more about her and why he would do that.'

Brandt watched as she leaned her head back, brought the jug to her lips and drank from it. For a moment he got lost in the graceful arch of her neck and the way her lips encircled the jug's opening. He shook himself free of the lustful thoughts rising within him at the sight.

'I wish to know that, too. I asked your father what had turned him against my father and he refused to answer me.'

'When did you ask him that? Did he come to you here?'

She stood then and held out the container to him. Her grip on it failed and he caught her hand and the jug in his. He lingered in letting her go, but when he released her and took the mead back, she began pacing. As she did when nervous or worried.

'He did. Not long after I asked you to tell him I wanted to speak to him. I suspect it was just before he set you off to spy on me and interrogate me.'

Brandt watched her movements slow until she sat once more on the stool in the corner. He drank another mouthful. 'He asked me questions, but gave no answers to mine.' He smiled grimly at her. 'So, about Kolga Olafsdottir.'

Brandt explained what he could about his mother and her older sister. That his father had courted Kolga first, with his eye on Maerr, only to push her aside for her more beautiful younger sister. That he laid claim to Maerr and the lands of Kolga's father in spite of her stronger claim and made certain she could not defend her rights to them. That even when she married and eventually had one child, that child was weak and should have been exposed for the gods' decision.

'Your cousin Eithr holds the throne now. With my father's help and backing?'

'Aye.' He fought the urge to spit in the dirt. 'When my father was killed, I went to claim the lands and throne. My brothers backed me, but we had no idea that this plot went much deeper and farther than simple assassinations.'

'Treason?' she asked. She put her elbow on her leg and placed her hand under her chin, watching him. Brandt sat on the pallet.

'Treason and personal treachery.'

'My father?'

'Well, when I made my claim, other jarls and land-owners accused my father of being a traitor. I think the King had difficulty believing their allegations, but we had no one and no way to refute their claims. Some said he'd approached them about overthrowing Harald. Others said he paid them to back him. And so on.' He shrugged.

'We'd heard nothing of the sort before and were caught unawares. By the time we realised how deep the conspiracy was, we were called outlaws by the King, my father's claim to Maerr was wiped away and my aunt's son was given it all.' He stopped, meeting her gaze before telling her the last of it. 'With Thorfinn's support and backing, which the King demanded in order to grant him possession and rule. Your father did not hesitate in anything that day but to stand by his friend's sons and declare the truth.'

She nodded at him before holding out her hand for the mead as though she needed it to help her bear up under the truth.

'Have a care,' he said as he handed it to her. 'Some-one told me this is a potent batch.' Potent or not, she drank another mouthful of it and nodded.

'Kolga was present? Did she speak?'

'Kolga let others speak for her. She did answer the King's questions, twisting every word spoken by oth-ers and shaping the truth to fit her goal.'

Neither spoke then and the silence grew between them. He could see her thinking over his words. Had she truly no idea of how this had come about? Now it was his turn to drink and he did. Though he should keep his wits about him when with her or he might do something stupid or senseless.

Like kiss her again. Or touch her.

Or peel off every layer of her garments to find her body beneath them. And then kiss her in every place he could touch, too.

He shook his head and put the stopper back in the jug, stashing it in the small space between the pallet and the wall. He'd had enough this night. And from the drowsy way her eyes fluttered, so had Katla.

'What did your father tell you of the matter? I do not remember you being there.' He frowned then, re-alising something else. 'I do not remember you being at their wedding either.'

'I was at neither one,' she confessed. 'Nor my sister. The marriage and his backing of Eithr were complete surprises to me.'

'He never told you he was marrying again?' She shook her head. 'How did you learn of it?' What a shock that must have been to her. But then, he'd left his daughter behind to live here even after her mother had died.

'He brought her here for the winter after they married. Eithr came with them. No announcement really. Just an introduction to her as my stepmother and she took over in my stead. All the duties I oversaw, she controlled.'

'You were young then. Had your father questioned your abilities before that?'

'Nay.' One word and yet it was imbued with all the sadness in the world. He could imagine her hurt. And, worse, Kolga was not a kind woman. Indeed, she was a cold and cruel woman to anyone but her son and her seizure of control would have been harshly done.

'This was five years ago?' Brandt tried to remember the way things had played out in Maerr. He had not even married Ingrid yet.

'We spent the winter here and then went back north in the spring for my marriage.' She was up and pacing after that. Her first husband who should have died terribly. 'My father allowed Kolga to choose him instead of honouring the promise he made to my mother that her eldest daughter would marry someone from Katanes. Our custom is that the lands move through the mother's family.'

That was not how it worked in the Norse lands. It moved from father to son or to the victors in a conflict. Only a strong man with strong sons could hope to keep control of his lands or titles among their people. That had been Sigurd's plan, but then…

'You lived with your father then?' He could not remember news of her marriage or that she had moved to the north with Thorfinn. Then he remembered that he had been getting married himself around that time. Thorfinn attended his marriage feast with his aunt and it had caused much strife between Sigurd and his friend.

'Aye, for those first few months. Though Trygg protested and wished for us to live with his family, my father insisted on our staying. With Kolga's backing, though, Trygg forced me to move with him.'

From the bleak and pained expression on her face,

she was remembering those times. Brandt retrieved the jug and gave it to her again. This time, she drank mouthful after mouthful until he pulled it away.

'One of us needs to walk out of here in a short while without help,' he said.

'You know, that was the last nice thing my father ever did for me.' Her voice softened and the lost look of despair left her eyes.

'Marrying you off to Trygg?' Brandt was confused, yet Katla seemed intent. She shook her head and began to wobble a bit. Brandt stepped closer and held her arms to keep her from falling over. Mayhap he should not have offered her the mead?

'Nay. Killing him for me.'

Brandt could not help the dark laugh that escaped then at the ease with which she accused her father of murder. He needed more effort to keep her standing. The stool would never hold her upright so he eased them over to the pallet and sat down, guiding her to sit next to him.

Rather than sitting up, she leaned against him, pressing her very warm and curved body to his. She would have fallen over if he'd not lifted his arm around her shoulders and held her. Even then, she rubbed her head on his arm and settled in as though getting comfortable in his embrace. Indeed, she wrapped her arm around his waist and let out a sigh.

'Why do you think he killed Trygg?' he asked. He hoped to keep her attention on their discussion and not on how close to his rampant flesh her hand now rested. Lifting her head, she smiled at him.

lantern she'd brought with her. They were long, muscular, soft-skinned, as he pushed the cloth out of his way and caressed them.

Her sigh echoed around them and filled the chamber, making him forget for just then that he was in a prison. The sheer pleasure in the sounds she uttered drove him on. Slowly, while yet meeting her gaze, he moved his hand to the top of her thighs, massaging one and then the other until her legs relaxed open for him. Though her gown yet covered them from his sight, he slid his fingers into the curls slowly, awaiting her reaction. He palmed her mound and slid one finger deeper within. Her mouth opened and the moan made him even harder. His flesh throbbed against her hip.

As he pressed into her woman's flesh, he kissed her, possessing her mouth as his hand possessed her core. She arched into his hand, and he added a second finger to tease and rub the folds. Soon, she rode his hand as he wished her to ride his flesh and he pleasured her, swallowing the moans and sighs of her arousal in his own mouth. Shallow, then deep. Light, then harder and faster until she was ready.

He felt her body tighten and felt the heat pour from her core as she reached satisfaction. She clutched at his shoulder as her body was rocked by wave after wave of pleasure. And all he could do was watch the expression of wonderment and disbelief and completion as it flitted across her expressive green eyes. He watched her mouth open as she panted shallow breaths. It took a bit of time for her eyes to lose their dream-like

'I had not truly believed it until you mentioned the others killed, or almost killed, on his ships. Trygg had kept his rage and violence hidden well until one night during a feast and my father witnessed it.'

She brushed her hair out of her face and grabbed hold of his belt. Fierce desire and heat poured through him as her hand slid back and forth along his belt. Brandt took hold of her hand and moved it to her lap. Gods, but he only had so much control!

'And your father?' he asked, clearing his throat that grew tight with the need to taste her.

'Oh, he took Trygg on a voyage to the west and when he returned, he told me that Trygg had fallen over the side of the ship while drunk.'

'Convenient.'

'A miracle sent by the gods,' she whispered. When he met her gaze, he suspected she was not speaking of her husband's untimely yet convenient death. Her green eyes shimmered as she lifted her face nearer to his. 'Kiss me.'

Two words that his entire body heard and responded to in the time between two beats of his heart.

'Katla,' he said as the better side of him regained control, 'we should not.'

'Kiss me, Brandt.' She turned in his arms and slid her hands up into his hair, pulling it free from the leather strips that bound it. 'Kiss me.'

And so he did. Gods help him, he kissed her.

Chapter Thirteen

He swore a silent oath he would not take her.

He swore another that he could stop himself.

The third oath he swore was that he would stop lying to himself about making promises to the gods. Especially when they concerned Katla Thorfinnsdottir.

She turned her soft, inviting body in his arms as he met her lips. Brandt wrapped his arms around her as their mouths touched and pulled her up on to his lap. Instead of shifting away from his hardened cock, she pressed her hip against it. The surge of pleasure and desire that flowed through him at that small contact nearly undid him. Brandt slid one arm behind her and held her head in his hand, keeping her face close to his.

When she opened her lips and he touched her tongue with his, her body simply melted into him. The sweet and heady taste of mead and something else that was only Katla awaited him within. And he tasted her, over and over, until she moaned against his lips.

All soft. All curves. All heated, even through their

garments. As he deepened the kiss, she began to rock on his lap. He held on to her hip at first, then let his hand glide along over her belly and up until he reached the fullness of her breast.

She gasped and opened her eyes, but when he slid his thumb over the tip of it, her eyes drifted closed and she pressed into his palm. He caressed and rubbed, enjoying the feel of her in his grasp. Her response fuelled his need for more and the way she clung to him, shifting until he could caress more of her, gave him the sign that she welcomed his touch.

The touch of an enemy.

The touch of a man after she'd only known brutality.

She lifted her face for a moment and his hand stilled on her breast. A smile that was temptation plain and simple and the sight of her kiss-swollen lips made him want more. But he would not trespass. Whether a widow, whether previously bedded or not, he would not be another man who forced himself or his attentions on her. That noble thought melted away as she covered his hand with her own and began to guide him.

When he slid his hand over her belly and could touch the place where her legs met, she kissed him. If he could have caught on fire, he would have. Her mouth was relentless in tasting him now and he let his hand move as hers followed, urging him lower and urging him on.

Brandt lifted his head to watch her face as he pulled free of her hand and began gathering the length of her gown in his. He could not help but look and admire as her legs were exposed to his view by the light of the

garments. As he deepened the kiss, she began to rock on his lap. He held on to her hip at first, then let his hand glide along over her belly and up until he reached the fullness of her breast.

She gasped and opened her eyes, but when he slid his thumb over the tip of it, her eyes drifted closed and she pressed into his palm. He caressed and rubbed, enjoying the feel of her in his grasp. Her response fuelled his need for more and the way she clung to him, shifting until he could caress more of her, gave him the sign that she welcomed his touch.

The touch of an enemy.

The touch of a man after she'd only known brutality.

She lifted her face for a moment and his hand stilled on her breast. A smile that was temptation plain and simple and the sight of her kiss-swollen lips made him want more. But he would not trespass. Whether a widow, whether previously bedded or not, he would not be another man who forced himself or his attentions on her. That noble thought melted away as she covered his hand with her own and began to guide him.

When he slid his hand over her belly and could touch the place where her legs met, she kissed him. If he could have caught on fire, he would have. Her mouth was relentless in tasting him now and he let his hand move as hers followed, urging him lower and urging him on.

Brandt lifted his head to watch her face as he pulled free of her hand and began gathering the length of her gown in his. He could not help but look and admire as her legs were exposed to his view by the light of the lantern she'd brought with her. They were long, muscular, soft-skinned, as he pushed the cloth out of his way and caressed them.

Her sigh echoed around them and filled the chamber, making him forget for just then that he was in a prison. The sheer pleasure in the sounds she uttered drove him on. Slowly, while yet meeting her gaze, he moved his hand to the top of her thighs, massaging one and then the other until her legs relaxed open for him. Though her gown yet covered them from his sight, he slid his fingers into the curls slowly, awaiting her reaction. He palmed her mound and slid one finger deeper within. Her mouth opened and the moan made him even harder. His flesh throbbed against her hip.

As he pressed into her woman's flesh, he kissed her, possessing her mouth as his hand possessed her core. She arched into his hand, and he added a second finger to tease and rub the folds. Soon, she rode his hand as he wished her to ride his flesh and he pleasured her, swallowing the moans and sighs of her arousal in his own mouth. Shallow, then deep. Light, then harder and faster until she was ready.

He felt her body tighten and felt the heat pour from her core as she reached satisfaction. She clutched at his shoulder as her body was rocked by wave after wave of pleasure. And all he could do was watch the expression of wonderment and disbelief and completion as it flitted across her expressive green eyes. He watched her mouth open as she panted shallow breaths. It took a bit of time for her eyes to lose their dream-like appearance and he knew the exact moment when she saw him once more.

'Brandt.' His name came out on a breathy whisper.

He moved his fingers and she gasped, pressing her legs together and trapping his hand. She was soft and hot when he found the wet folds of her flesh. He smiled at her body's reaction to his touch.

'Katla,' he whispered back. He kissed her, barely rubbing their lips together. 'More?'

He could spend hours doing this. Touching and caressing her until she moaned or screamed out her body's release. He would prefer the light of day so he could see if her skin blushed with pleasure. He would prefer it to be on a bed of furs next to a roaring fire so he could peel off her clothes and expose all of her to his sight. How many times could he bring her to completion in one night? How many ways could he arouse her and tease her flesh before they both grew exhausted?

Katla smiled at him as she tightened the muscles around his fingers. He'd leaned down closer to her when the sound of the door closing at the end of the hall startled them both. He removed his hand, tugged her gown back into place and helped her stand. Glancing around the cell, there was no place for her to hide. Whoever now strode down the corridor would discover her.

'Here,' he said as he lifted the fur and blankets from the pallet. 'Lie down.' He helped her lie down on the far side of the pallet and tossed a blanket over her, covering her from head to toe. 'Do not make a sound.'

Brandt climbed in next to her, turning on his side to

shield the sight of her. In the darkness, she would not be seen. Unless someone entered the cell. Darkness? Gods damn, but the lantern still burned. Too late, for the person approaching reached the door. Brandt shuffled the other blankets over him and waited.

'Who is in there?' Alfaran called out. Brandt waited, purposely not answering him at first. 'Sigurd's son! Wake up!' He waited long enough to give the appearance of being asleep, but not so long that the commander would be tempted to enter.

'I am awake. Is it time to work?' Brandt remained on his side, praying this would work to protect Katla.

'Are you alone?' Alfaran asked. 'I thought I heard you speaking to someone.'

'I talk in my sleep,' he said, rubbing his face. 'Nightmares and such.'

'Where did that lantern come from?' Still no sound of a key being tried. Which was good because the door was unlocked.

'One of the servants left it when they took the remnants of my supper. I confess I did not call them back for it.'

Alfaran considered his words. Brandt waited to see if he would come in—if he had another reason for his visit. Katla lay motionless behind him. He could feel the warmth of her body close to his, but she made no sound.

Brandt did not realise he was holding his breath until Alfaran walked away. He let it out, but cautioned Katla not to move with a touch of his hand. To be certain it was safe, he waited until after the door at the end of the corridor had closed and silence settled back in this lower part of the keep.

Katla lay next to him, not moving, not making a sound and just barely breathing, as she listened to Brandt and Alfaran. And she prayed to any of the gods who would listen to her for protection. Not that she deserved it. Had she truly just thrown herself at this man and begged for his kiss? His touch? Even now she could feel the burn of embarrassment fill her cheeks.

He'd kissed her, if that could be called kissing. It was more like possession. More like claiming a part of her she did not know existed. More like the complete surrender of her soul. She shivered then, realising that not only had she invited it, she had relished it, giving herself over to the pleasure of something that had never interested her before.

Trygg had kissed her during their marriage. Arni had tried and succeeded several times already. And yet, none of those experiences could compare. Those were assaults. Attempts to control and overpower and humiliate her.

Brandt's kisses invited her. To passion. To explore. To accept. His mouth and tongue tempted her to… more. Even now her lips were swollen from those kisses and she wanted to begin again.

Her body throbbed as she lay next to his warmth and strength, still craving his touch. He'd given her such pleasure without seeing to his body's demands. Oh, he'd been ready, for she'd felt the proof of his arousal thick and hard against her hip. Yet, he'd not even attempted to take his lust out on her. Trygg never wasted time on touching or caressing her during their bed play. Arni promised only pain and torment. And here, her enemy, a man who she should fear and hate, brought her satisfaction she'd never experienced before.

And he protected her from discovery with his own body.

Alfaran had walked away and they lay in silence as his footsteps disappeared down the corridor. Brandt's hand on her hip kept her silent and still for now. Was it a trick on Alfaran's part to pretend to leave? Well, she would not take that chance.

If she admitted the truth to herself, she was not ready to leave the warmth of his nearness yet. Other truths flitted about and she was not ready for those either. Instead, she waited for his sign that it was safe. He shifted and drew the blankets off her face.

'I think you should wait a bit longer before you leave.'

Had her disappointment shown on her face? He leaned back a little and examined her closely. Just before Alfaran's arrival, he'd offered her more and she discovered that she wanted it. Even if it meant doing the rest of it. She finally nodded.

'I—' she began.

'I—' he said at the same time. 'Go on.'

'You did not...' a slight shift against him revealed his flesh was still hard...and still very large. And ready '...take your pleasure.' Katla was so proud of the way the words came out smoothly.

He rolled from his side to his back and pushed his

loosened hair from his face. Had she insulted him somehow? Should she not have remarked on it? The silence that surrounded them was awkward somehow. He drew in long, deep breaths and let them out slowly as she watched. Was he trying to control his response? Had she angered him?

'I do not wish to take advantage of you, Katla.'

'You do not want to…do this?' she asked, swirling her finger in the direction of his manhood. He sucked in a breath so quickly that he choked on it. She waited until he stopped before speaking. 'I have never had a man do that to me before. Is it not a prelude to…that?'

Now, when she gestured towards his flesh with her hand, he choked without coughing. Was she wrong to be honest with him? She was a widow, after all, and it was not uncommon for women to seek out lovers if they did not want husbands. Her situation was not as simple as that, but in her father's—in Thorfinn's absence, and if she were discreet, no one would have spoken of it. He met her gaze then and she saw something akin to pity in their depths.

Katla pushed to sit up and shoved the blankets off her. She would not take pity from him. Not from anyone. Let him think what he would, she did not want to see that expression in his eyes. She got to her knees and crawled off the pallet without touching or moving over him. The chamber began to shift a bit around her as she stood and Katla reached out to try to regain her balance. He was at her side before she fell over.

'Here now,' he said, guiding her to the stool. 'You

have had more mead than I did and may not be ready
to walk out of here.'

She allowed his help for her head spun and threatened to topple her. Her body felt languid from the
amount of drink she'd imbibed and the overwhelming
pleasure and release she'd experienced at his hand. As
she watched, he crouched down before her, even while
he yet held her steady.

'Most times I prefer to find satisfaction in a woman's body,' he said softly. She could not meet his intense gaze and looked past him. 'But sometimes, giving
pleasure is enough.' When she did not reply or look at
him, he tugged on her hand to get her attention. 'If no
man has given you pleasure like that while seeking his
own, then he is not worthy of you.'

'Was not.'

He smiled at her, a grim half-smile, that told her
he knew to whom she referred. 'Nay, he was not. I am
glad he could not swim so well.'

Katla nodded and smiled back, relieved to be able to
share her feelings, even in a vague way, about Trygg's
death and departure from her life. When she would
have spoken, he placed his finger on her lips.

''Tis not that I do not want you, Katla. I do. I want
to take you over and over until we are exhausted by the
pleasure of it and can no longer move. I want to taste
every inch of you with my tongue and I want to touch
your skin, your mouth, your breasts, and especially
where my hand found the heat of you, with my mouth.'

His eyes dropped lower, gazing at the place between
her legs. She tightened her muscles against the sudden

awareness that pulsed within her. She could not breathe at his words. A man would do that?

'Aye, this man would.' She'd spoken the words aloud. His answer brought a wave of heat that shot through her, making her skin tight and the place where he'd touched throb. 'I would show you the way it can be between a man and a woman.'

She wanted it, him, too. For the first time since the reality of being married to Trygg had destroyed the anticipation of it all, she wanted him to join with her. To feel him on top of her, and over her, and...*in* her. Desire rose in her, rushing through her and making her breasts swell against the fabric of her gown. Would he put his mouth there, too? Without thought, her hands covered her breasts, seeking to ease the ache of it all.

'Aye, I will taste those, too,' he whispered. 'Your breasts will be the perfect mouthful for me.' A piercing need filled her woman's core and she stood up quickly. He stood as well, not moving away from her. The man towered over her and she had to lift her face to see his.

'Now?' she asked. 'Now,' she answered her own question. 'Now.'

'Sadly, you must go now, Katla. I doubt Alfaran will give up easily if he suspects your visits to me are for purposes other than what your father ordered. 'Tis getting too close to when we must escape to do anything to put your plan in danger.'

He was urging caution? He was trying to protect her? What kind of enemy did that? What kind of foe did not take every advantage of the situation or of those whom he called enemy? What kind of man was Brandt Sigurdsson?

An honourable man.

A man she could trust.

A man she could love if she was not careful of her feelings about him.

Katla nodded and stepped back slowly, keeping her balance this time as she moved. She took the lantern from him when he held it out to her and moved to the door.

'I will return on the morrow. We need to sort out when we will leave and how. And what to take and who.'

'Who? I thought it was you and your sister.'

'I am considering asking my aunt to flee with us.'

He was silent for a moment. 'Could she make the journey that we must make to escape?' He shook his head before she answered. 'That is what you must consider before asking her.'

'I will.'

Katla opened the door and found the key where she'd left it on the floor just outside. Turning back, she glanced up at him once more.

'Have a care around Alfaran, Katla. I do not trust him at all,' he urged her. 'I think he may be working with my aunt rather than for your father and, if I am correct, he is far more dangerous than I first thought.'

A chill coursed through her body that had little to do with the cold air in the dungeon and more to do with all the possible dangers she, they, faced. Only the realisation that she had an ally in this made her feel calm.

Even the overwhelming and obvious desire that showed in his eyes and expression and in his body had not terrified her. When Trygg had looked at her with lust, she had been immobilised with fear and the knowledge of what was to come. His awful battering of her body and soul tore her apart bit by bit. Every time he took her, he stole more and more of her confidence and joy. Never did he give her anything but pain and terror and heartbreak.

Yet when this Viking enemy gazed at her, his eyes filled with frank desire and need, her body responded to him. He made her want him in the same way. He brought her pleasure and, for the first time in her womanhood, he made her want more.

Want him. Want more with him.

As she made her way to her chambers, Katla was struck with sadness as she also understood that no matter what she wanted, he could never be hers, for he was destined to die in his battle for honour and vengeance. The odds were against him and they were even worse if he was trying to live through this. But he was not. He knew what and who was against him and he would follow the path he'd chosen in spite of that, to the death.

An honourable man.

A man she could trust.

A man she could love.

A man she could never have.

Chapter Fourteen

Their next encounter was an awkward one and, worse, one that happened in the yard while many others watched. Katla was carrying a basket to one of the storage sheds in the yard and was not paying heed to those working or walking. The memories of Brandt's touch and caresses last night had haunted her thoughts all through the day and she'd been lost in them when she walked into him.

Careless and foolish, her impact knocked the boards that he carried on his shoulder from his control and sent them toppling on to the men around him who guarded his every step. He'd regained his balance and helped her to steady herself when she met his gaze and it sent her spiralling into need and desire that was so strong and immediate it frightened her.

They stared for a scant moment, but it was too long and it caught the attention of too many. The guards, angry over Brandt's seeming clumsiness and now frank appraisal of their lord's daughter, attacked him, pushing and punching him as they tried to force him back to work.

His laugh, full and loud and filled with a strange joy, sent chills through her. As she turned to watch, he laughed once more and then fought back. He moved around them, never once straying more than a pace in any direction, taking the guards on as they moved closer. One went down in a crumpled heap from a punch to his jaw. Another fell away, clutching his chest after a powerful blow to his ribs cracked several. One guard jumped on Brandt's back and threw his arm around his neck, trying to cut off his breathing. Brandt backed him into another, freeing up the hold, and threw the man to the ground, knocking him out with a strong blow.

Katla held her breath now as their battle continued and it took a bit of time and attention for her to realise that this had changed into something else. More guards approached, but did not join into the fray until others had been knocked out or forced away. All through it, Brandt called to them, insulting them and goading them into the mayhem. He was…enjoying it.

Glancing from him to the other men watching or waiting their turn, she could see that this was not a fight based on threat or danger, it was based on that male need to show off and to fight whenever possible. When a dispute could be settled with words or discussion, she'd noticed that men lost interest. If it could be solved with fists, they could not get in the middle of it fast enough to suit them. That was happening right before her eyes.

A contest of male pride. A battle to prove nothing more than that their manhood was bigger than another's.

Katla took advantage of the cheering crowd that surrounded the prisoner and the battle to get to the shed and hide away some of the supplies they would need for their escape. Bit by bit, she'd been bringing things— sacks of dried food, skins of water or ale, winter cloaks, even a weapon or two—here so they were ready and close at hand when needed. She shoved them behind barrels that stood in the centre of the shed, out of sight, until they would retrieve them as they left the keep.

Soon, the yard quietened and Katla returned to see what was happening. Her heart pounded when she saw Brandt's next challenger. As his presence became known, the crowd stopped cheering and those waiting to fight dropped away. When Brandt finished off his opponent, with only a split lip and cut on his chin to show for it, he turned to find Alfaran behind him.

'Do you come to test yourself against me, Alfaran?'

Alfaran's grim smile spoke of a true threat as he nodded and walked closer. The crowd widened in its circle as her father's commander, a brutal warrior skilled in combat and control, approached. Brandt rolled his shoulders and set his stance, motioning him to come with a wave of his hand.

'You should not have tried to escape, son of Sigurd.'

'Only a blind man would say such a thing, Alfaran. They all know I did not,' Brandt answered, nodding at those gathered around him.

'I saw you.'

'Will that be your claim when Thorfinn discovers me dead?' Brandt smiled and it was one that Katla hoped he never directed at her. A tremor of fear shook her body and she clutched her hands to keep them steady. She fought to keep silent for distracting him now would result in someone's death. 'Come, then,' he called out. 'Your men put up a good fight. Let us see if their commander can as well.'

Anger raced through her. Why? Why did he torment and goad Alfaran into this? Was Brandt strong enough to withstand the fury of the commander now that his honour and his skills had been questioned in front of his men? She wanted to scream and stamp her feet. If he was injured, would he survive? Would he be able to claim his vengeance if Alfaran took him down?

It was too late to do anything but watch, for Alfaran charged Brandt, sword drawn and death in his gaze. Hissing came from the men as they showed their disdain for the use of a weapon when none had been raised. Katla was stunned by the act of the men, for they had a sense of fairness that their commander did not. In the blink of an eye, this fight went from good-natured to until death. This was not about male pride, this was about killing his prisoner.

And, rather than dropping the lethal weapon and using his fists, Alfaran swung it, trying to kill Brandt. Men shifted away, giving both of them more room to move. If anyone thought to intervene, the swift strokes of the deadly sword kept them out of it. She searched for any sign of her father's arrival and found none.

Brandt dived out of the way of one blow and landed

in the mud and ice. Alfaran followed with a slicing swing, but Brandt was fast, rolling out of the way. As he regained his feet, a sword slid across the clearing towards him. Katla tried to see who'd passed it to him and could not. When Alfaran saw it in his grasp he cursed aloud. Wasting not a moment, the commander chased Brandt. When Brandt stopped and turned suddenly to face his opponent with a smile, Katla knew he would be fine.

With a sword now in his hand they were evenly matched and this would be a battle which either could win. Alfaran, certainly, had more recent training and practice, while Brandt's reputation and skills as a warrior were strong, hence all the men who'd wanted to fight him so they could say they had.

'What is going on here?' Her aunt's voice broke into her concentration and Katla found the older woman standing at her side. How long she'd been watching, Katla did not know.

'Alfaran is trying to kill Brandt.'

'But Thorfinn ordered otherwise,' Alpia said. 'Why would the commander disobey an order like that? And before so many witnesses.'

Without taking her gaze off the continuing fight, Katla shrugged. 'It was simply a challenge between the men and Brandt until Alfaran arrived and accused Brandt of trying to escape.' Katla sighed. ''Twas my fault, I fear. I stumbled into his path which caused him to drop what he was carrying on to the guards. They challenged him. He accepted.'

'As men do,' Alpia said.

'Aye. As men are wont to do. But this escalated when Alfaran made his accusation—which everyone here knows is a lie. Then he went after him with a sword.'

'And how will this end?' her aunt asked.

'Unless my father intervenes—' Katla looked over the crowd towards the door of the keep—the closed door—and shook her head '—when one of them dies.'

'You do not look worried, Niece.' Her aunt bumped her own hip into Katla's. 'Why is that?'

'I do not know.'

'Are you certain of the outcome or certain that you hope the Viking wins this battle?'

'I—' As she was about to tell her aunt that she had faith in Brandt's ability to win in this, something odd occurred to her.

Something that Brandt had said made sense to Katla—that he suspected Alfaran worked more for his aunt than for Katla's father. It made sense of why the man would want him dead. If Brandt remained alive to challenge his right to Maerr, Kolga's sins would be revealed. If Alfaran worked for her, he would need to ensure that did not happen for his own misdeeds, along with everyone else involved in their plot, would be exposed.

And that meant that since Alfaran had decided his course, this course, of action, he would see it through by whatever means he need use, whether fair or foul. A hidden dagger. An unknown or unseen co-conspirator. A trap of some kind that would leave Brandt vulnerable. She searched the area, watching for some sign of one of those.

'What are you looking for, Katla? The fight is over there,' her aunt said, nodding in the direction of Brandt and Alfaran.

'Aunt Alpia, if you wanted to win a fight by any means, how would you do it?'

'I am no help in matters like this,' she answered. 'I would avoid the fight completely.'

'And if you could not or did not wish to avoid it? How could you win?'

'Help. I would have others to help me in subtle ways.'

Almost as if she'd directed this scene, someone along the edges of the crowd tripped Brandt. The crowd yelled their displeasure, but he'd lost his balance and tumbled across the clearing.

'Like that?' Katla looked at her aunt, who nodded in reply.

'Aye.'

Another man seemed to back into the fight by accident and Brandt shifted to avoid hitting him, giving Alfaran an opening to strike. If she had not been watching closely, she would have thought it wholly part of the flow of battle. But she had been observing and knew it was done apurpose.

'We must stop this.' Katla saw no sign that her father would arrive in time. Brandt was struggling more as this fight went on. If Alfaran had accomplices, Brandt would die. 'Now, Aunt. Follow me.'

If her distraction had started it, then another one must end it. She made her way through the ring of people and, when almost to the clearing where they fought, she stopped. With a quick glance at the older woman, Katla spun around, let out a scream and fell to the ground in between the two men.

And she prayed that they would stop rather than step over her to continue!

Alpia played her part well, calling out and gaining attention as Katla lay unmoving. Daring to peek, she watched as Brandt tossed his sword to one of the guards and held up his hands. The entire yard quieted then, waiting for Alfaran's next move. Her father broke into it instead.

'Alfaran, have the guards take my daughter inside and take the prisoner to his cell.'

Men and women scurried back to their chores, trying to make themselves less visible and less a target for their lord's anger. Katla stirred and opened her eyes as some of the guards lifted her from the ground. 'What happened?' she asked.

Whether her father believed her or not, she could not guess, but he allowed her action to go unchallenged. Alfaran was not that fortunate. Would he chastise his commander if he knew the man was working for his wife? Or mayhap Brandt had it wrong? Mayhap Alfaran worked for both of them in carrying out their plans?

'Oh, my dear Katla,' her aunt cried out. 'Thank the gods you have awakened. Are you well?'

'I grew dizzy and everything began to spin around before me.' She let the men aid her in standing, brushing her gown down and flicking some of the hay and mud from the bottom of it. Careful not to be too insistent, she nodded at the men and then at Thorfinn. 'I think I need to rest.' With a stiff nod, he gave his permission and Katla and Alpia left.

Just before they entered the keep, she heard her father call out, 'Alfaran, if you are in need of a fight, I will give it to you.'

The clanging of their swords rang through the yard now and was met with complete and utter silence. No one cheered or called out or whispered as their lord sought to discipline an underling who had disobeyed him. Thorfinn's word was law and he would take action when he needed to. How would Alfaran react to this? He'd sworn allegiance to her father. He'd done Thorfinn's bidding for years. Would he acquiesce and allow her father to win easily which would offer an insult? Or would he fight to win, unseating Thorfinn from his place here? He'd looked in fine fighting condition when Brandt had challenged him, though he had not the motivation to win that his opponent did. Now? Now she wondered at what would happen.

Though Katla wanted to remain, she knew better than to try this time. She followed Alpia even as the older woman escorted her to her own chamber. Once they walked inside it, she understood why. Alpia's chamber had a small window that opened with a view of the yard. Once the chamber door was closed and the guards gone, they hastened to it and opened it enough so they could watch.

Thorfinn Bjornsson fought like a man possessed. His commander did not stand a chance of winning this. When he managed to force the sword from Alfaran's grip and send it flying, an expression of true fear covered the man's face. That was something Katla had never seen in her life. Thorfinn sheathed his sword and knocked him to the ground with his fists, not stopping until Alfaran did not move.

Katla could not tell if he'd killed his commander or not until the man's foot moved. Thorfinn crouched down then and spoke only to Alfaran. Whatever he said took no time at all, for Thorfinn stood, glared at everyone still watching or standing around and returned to the keep. Katla stepped back and closed the window, stunned by everything that she'd just witnessed. Stumbling across the chamber, she sat on her aunt's bed and shook her head.

'What madness is this?'

'I guess the prisoner is recovered from his injuries.'

'Alpia? Aye, you know he is recovered.' Sometimes her aunt did not make sense. She seemed to answer questions having nothing to do with what was asked, but rather ones of her own choosing on other matters completely.

'I think you should ask him to help you escape.'

Of all the things that her aunt could have said at that moment, this was not one she'd considered. And the fact that it was exactly what she'd already done made Katla worry that others had thought the same.

'He is the prisoner, Aunt. Not I.'

Alpia walked to her side, sat down and took one of Katla's hand in hers. She stroked Katla's cheek then and shook her head, her eyes filled with sadness.

'You are more prisoner than anyone I know, Niece.

More than your mother was when the Norse arrived on our shores interested in more than just pillaging and destruction. If you remain here and are forced to marry that man...' She paused and took a breath. 'I know what awaits you if you marry him. And I cannot bear to watch it happen.'

They'd never spoken of her coming marriage or her fate like this before. Katla had made certain to only say aloud the right words. Words that accepted her father's dominion over her. Words that accepted his choices and his declarations and orders. Words that would protect her sister, if not herself.

'I have remembered a cousin who lives in the south, near Inbhir Nis. She moved with her husband a few years ago.'

The words hung out in the space between them— Alpia not elaborating and Katla taking them as she meant them. Her aunt would be an ally in her plan. Katla was going to explain when a knock came on the door. A guard summoned her and her needle and thread to her father's chamber.

'We will speak later, Katla,' Alpia promised as she opened the door.

Katla hurried back to her chamber to get her basket and then made her way to her father's room. Mayhap by the time she left here, she would stop thinking of him as her father?

'Come.'

She pushed open the door and found Thorfinn sitting at the table, drinking and bleeding from a deep gash on his forehead at the place where his hair began. He alternated between pressing a cloth to the cut and taking mouthfuls of whatever filled the cup. When she got closer, she could see it was that same mead she'd taken to Brandt only last night.

'Have a care with that. 'Tis a potent batch,' she said.

A servant followed her in with the bowl of hot water she'd sent for. Placing it by the hearth, Katla poured a little into another bowl and added some herbs from her basket. Once the servant left, she approached him, carrying the hot water to cleanse the wound, so she could get a better view of it.

He hissed at her touch, but did not move or stop her from her work. Soon, she could see the edges of the wound and applied pressure until the worst of the bleeding stopped. While he drank more, she retrieved her needle and thread and waited for his sign to begin. He placed his cup on the table and nodded.

As she placed one careful stitch after another, it struck her that she had not accepted Thorfinn's part in Kolga's treachery. That he had willingly entered into some arrangement with her to kill his old friend and that man's family. Something bothered her even as she understood he was as ruthless and harsh as he needed or wanted to be. Somehow, the killing of women and children at a wedding under a truce did not fit him.

That did not mean he was innocent of it all.

But the feeling that he would need a strong, very strong, reason to join in such a plan was one she could not ignore or explain. Not without knowing what such a reason could be. As she sewed the wound closed, Katla listened to his even breathing. How could she find out more from him? Would he speak to her on such matters at all or would he ignore her words as he was happy to be getting rid of her shortly?

'Does Alfaran know the outlaw, Father?' she asked, keeping her voice even and low. She did not miss a stitch as she spoke.

'Why do you ask?'

'He seems ready to disobey you over him. I wondered if there was bad blood between them.'

She was taking a chance, a huge dangerous chance, bringing it up this way, but she wanted to know how deep in this her father was.

'I know not.'

She did not press then, only continued to sew the edges of his wound. About five more were needed now. She tried to stay calm as she tied off the thread. When she finished and turned away to get the ointment needed for the injury, he grabbed her wrist.

'Why do you ask this?'

'Brandt...the prisoner told me that Alfaran visits him below.'

'What?' He turned on his chair to face her. 'For what purpose?'

'The prisoner said he comes in the night to taunt him. But he mentioned...' She paused then, waiting for his reaction.

'Brandt mentioned what?' He stood, then sat down once more when she carried the unguent towards him. 'What did he tell you?'

'He thinks, for some reason known to him, that Alfaran serves your wife more than he serves you.'

If she could come up with a way to describe his expression in those next moments, she would have. Incredulous. Suspicious. Confused. Surprised. So many emotions crossed his face and filled his eyes in such a short time. Katla noticed the moment when he drew himself back under control and showed her nothing.

The most surprising thing she had not seen was anger. The other missing reaction was guilt. She'd seen no guilt in his eyes as he considered Brandt's accusation.

'What else did he say about Alfaran?' he asked.

'Nothing else. He only spoke that suspicion.'

She finished up by putting the medicament and a clean bandage on his head. It would not last; he would remove the bandage before setting foot outside his chamber and more likely when the next person, be they kith, kin or servant, arrived at his door. Her duty done, she gathered up her supplies and packed up her basket, tossing the used water into the bottom of the hearth where it hissed and disbursed.

'You will tell me if he says anything more.' An order.

'Certainly, Father.'

'Do you speak to him each night?'

'Most nights, Father.'

'Does anyone else know that you go to the dungeon? The guards?'

'I wait until the guards have locked up for the night before I go. No one knows.' She glanced at him then.

'Alfaran may have seen me leaving the other night. I try to be careful and hide myself in the shadows.' Would he strike out at her for carelessness? When he did not move, other than to take another drink of the mead, she wondered if she was dismissed. 'Have you need of anything else?'

Another strange expression met her gaze then. She tried to read, it but could not, for, in the time it took her to see it, it disappeared. Being hopeful in spite of her experience, Katla thought it might have been a plea for forgiveness, but what possible sin would Thorfinn Bjornsson want her to forgive?

'Nay. Just tell me anything he says. You may go.'

As she walked back to the kitchen area where she kept a small room to make her unguents and potions, Katla understood one thing.

She was not convinced her father was a partner in Kolga's plot against Sigurd and his family. Oh, he was involved and most likely guilty of many sins, but it was not his plot, his treachery. The more she thought on what had happened, the more she was also convinced that this had all the markings of a woman seeking revenge for wrongs done her.

A man like Thorfinn, or Sigurd for that matter, when he felt slighted or insulted in any way would issue a challenge or simply and directly attack the other to seek redress. Straightforward. In their face. With all the men who swore fealty to him at his back.

But if you wanted revenge and did not have 'men at your back', what did you do? Who would not have men who rose at their call?

A woman.

A woman who would use others to gain her ends. A woman who would hide her plan and divide it up so others could carry out bits of it without being the wiser for the whole.

Blackmailing her own sister for non-existent transgressions and using the pieces of gold and silver she demanded for silence to pay others to do her work for her.

Arranging to split up those who could make sense of it all, sending the five brothers first into hiding and then having them declared outlaws.

Making certain that the man who had scorned and insulted her died first and then ruining his family's claim.

Putting her weakling son on a throne and getting Katla's father to support that action.

Too personal. Too hidden. Too sneaky for a man.

But exactly how a woman would have to accomplish something this nefarious.

A woman like Kolga Olafsdottir.

Her father's wife.

Chapter Fifteen

All in all, it had not been a bad morning.

Or a bad night before it when he remembered Katla coming apart at his touch.

The guards shuffled him inside and he did not resist. Truth be told, he was exhausted. Exhausted, but exhilarated.

It had been a long time since he'd fought so many men like that and that last time had been when all his brothers were still together. A little chaos in the midst of a feast that sent them brawling out of their longhouse and into the village centre. He could not even remember the cause of it now—too much drinking, more than likely—but it had only taken a few punches before the whole thing rippled out and consumed those present.

Old, young. Sober, drunk. It had mattered not that night. All that had mattered was punching or being punched until one or no one was left standing. Some were felled by others, but many ended up on the ground due to simple drunkenness! As he watched the door to his cell close, he thought that mayhap only Rurik had stood that night. His half-brother could both hold his drink and stand his ground.

Those were good memories.

The guard turned the key and called out an insult as he walked away, making Brandt realise he must be one of the men he'd fought before Alfaran's appearance. Brandt insulted the guard back and heard him laugh his way down the corridor. Enemies or not, they'd fought like men of honour and it had been a good thing.

Until Alfaran had turned it into an ambush.

Not a single person in that yard would say he had been trying to escape. Not one. Even the guards around him had stood between him and the gates. And Brandt had made it clear to Thorfinn and to Katla that he wanted the chance to fight for his family's honour. A man with that goal, that need, did not escape. He stayed, as Brandt had done.

Well, he smiled then; once he got Thorfinn's daughters out and away he would return.

Alfaran's attack made it clearer than ever to him that the man served his Aunt Kolga. Though commander of Thorfinn's warriors, he looked out for his aunt's interests. And they both knew, as Thorfinn must, that Brandt being given a voice in this matter would uncover all manner of sins—some worthy of committing and others needing to be hidden away.

He paced the length of the chamber, still uncertain why Thorfinn not only allowed him to live, but helped him to live. He had prevented his men from killing him the first day. He had sent his daughter to see to his needs at great cost to her own health. He had aided in his recovery and then, under the guise of making him work, gave him the opportunity to rebuild his strength. Then he had fed him more and sent his daughter over and over to see to him—again in a disguised way so it did not look as though he was doing so.

And his recent actions pricked Brandt's curiosity even more. Oh, he did not mistake that he owed Katla yet again for saving his life. Her collapse might have fooled those watching because they were not paying heed to her as he did. That she fell directly between them with her aunt wailing to the heavens at the same moment interrupted the fight and made it impossible for Alfaran to continue his attack without killing his lord's daughter. Brandt had seen her watching through barely opened eyes as she waited for the results of her action and knew she was fine.

Then, Thorfinn stepped in—asserting his orders about Brandt in an unmistakable way that would let every person in Wik Castle know that his commander was being dishonourable. And disobedient. Something a strong man could not allow unless he wanted constant challenges to his right to rule. He'd been pulled aside and dragged in before he could see the outcome, but the look in Thorfinn's eyes when he spoke and drew his sword left no doubt in Brandt's mind that Thorfinn would be the victor.

The question that he could not answer was the reason behind it all.

If Thorfinn was guilty of planning and executing this treachery, why keep Brandt alive to expose his guilt? If he'd known about it, why would he seek such vengeance against a man he'd counted as a friend for so long? Had his father in some way betrayed Thorfinn and broken their friendship? The two men had been drawn apart in the years leading up to the massacre, for both were important men with many demands on their time—Sigurd with Maerr to rule and Thorfinn with his ships and trade.

Then, Thorfinn's marriage to Kolga had chilled things between him and Sigurd. Knowing now what he had not known then, Brandt understood more of the context behind it all. His aunt hated his father for what he'd taken from her. When she married his friend, it forced Sigurd away. But when had marrying a contrary woman soured a deep friendship such as theirs had been?

As the cold of the chamber began to seep into his weary body, Brandt retrieved the small jug of mead and drank a mouthful, wrapping himself in the cloak that the guard had tossed in with him.

All this thinking brought him back to a question that had never been asked or answered—why had Thorfinn married Kolga? He had no sons yet and she was no longer bearing children. Eithr was a sad heir who would never hold his throne without Thorfinn to defend it for him.

He shivered then and took another drink. He would have to be careful of this mead—it would steal his reason. Or his control.

So, why had Thorfinn not pursued a match with a different and much younger woman who would bear

him many sons? He was still a vigorous man, capable
of making sons who would make his claim even here
in Katanes a stronger one. He'd be foolish to leave a
daughter here, even one married to a Norseman, worse
if married to a local noble.

The flood of warriors being forced out of his kingdom by Harald who was consolidating his own power
and control was sending more and more south and west
seeking new lands of their own. A huge army had arrived in the lands of East Anglia, Mercia, Northumbria, and Wessex a few years ago and travelled the
countryside, taking lands and settling their way deep
into the territories of the Angles and the Saxons. But
that wave in the south did not protect these lands from
such an invasion.

So, only a strong warrior with strong sons stood a
chance of holding these lands for any time forward.

Sigurd's sons had stood high in the regard of that
King and had been safe from the pressure to leave their
homelands. They'd sworn allegiance to him and sworn
to fight for him. If only they'd known that his favour
was something lightly given and swiftly withdrawn.

So much of this made no sense to him.

He was missing something. Something critical to
the whole plan of it. Critical to why Thorfinn was a
part of it.

Brandt let out a foul curse and waited as it echoed
around him. None of that should have mattered. None
of it.

His father was dead. His wife and son were dead.

So many others died that terrible night. That was what mattered.

Thorfinn was part of it. That was what mattered.

Motives did not matter, only actions.

Whatever had driven Thorfinn to be part of this was not important. It did not matter.

But as he reached once more for that damn jug of mead and drank deeply of it, Brandt only knew it did. It did matter, even if he did not wish it to be so.

By the time darkness fell, he ached in places he'd forgotten could hurt. Yet the ache felt good, much like those first days when they'd put him to work in the yard had. The wounds he'd sustained on the first day were gone completely, other than the small puckered marking on his skin where the arrows had entered or gone through him.

Katla had worked her needle well.

He would not need that this day, for only a few scratches, shallow cuts and bruises were the results of his battles and Alfaran had been stopped before he could cause real, lasting damage. As he waited through the rest of the day, Brandt hoped she would come tonight. He wanted to talk about their plan and he had questions for her about the lands nearby and her father.

Would she answer them?

How far could he push before her innate loyalty took over and stopped her? Something within him was convinced she would not betray him and she was honest in her need for his help, yet he was still wary when it came to assisting his enemy's daughter.

* * *

Supper arrived with a surprise—two buckets of hot water and some soap—and he wasted no time in cleaning off the blood and muck from the wounds of the day's fighting. Though the light coming in through the small window at the end of the corridor was dim, it lasted longer each day, telling him that the time to act was coming soon.

Once the seas were safe enough, Kolga would sail south from Maerr. Since he'd arrived here in midwinter, no one could have urged her to travel faster or warned her of Brandt's presence here and his challenge. So, she would arrive here in no haste and with no inkling of what she faced.

He lay down on the pallet after he'd eaten, intent on sorting through the best way to get Thorfinn's daughters to safety.

The next time he opened his eyes, he was not alone.

'You snore.'

'Never!' he said, pushing up on his elbows and looking across the chamber at her. Katla rested her chin on her hand and smiled.

'And you call out in your sleep just as you told Alfaran you did.' He blushed then and she was drawn in by it.

'What did I say?' His words challenged her, but that blush gave away that he knew the truth of it—Brandt Sigurdsson talked in his sleep.

'I have been here for some time now and you have been snoring so loudly that you did not even hear me enter.' He had been deeply asleep, for she had spoken his name several times and nothing had roused him. 'Then you called out to your brothers, some of them by name.'

'Was it…?' Sadness entered his eyes then and she realised he must have been thinking it was a dream of the attack on Maerr.

'In truth, it sounded like you were fighting.' He smiled then and nodded.

'Another memory of earlier days.'

'Brought on by today's battles mayhap?'

'Mayhap.' When he smiled fully, she knew the memories were good ones.

'I was about to seek out my own bed.'

Partly she teased him, for he was breathtaking when he woke and she was intimidated by the image of pure masculinity he presented so close at hand. The chamber felt smaller to her and she wondered, for the first time, if this was a good idea after all. When he sat up and the blankets over him fell away, revealing his naked chest and stomach to her, her mouth went dry.

Katla tried to put her attention on something more mundane, searching his face for signs of new injuries. She failed at that as well for all she could see was his rugged good looks and the mouth that had haunted her dreams last night and her thoughts all through this day.

'I am glad you are here.'

'You are? Are you injured?' She stood and walked closer, bringing the lantern with her for a better view. She inspected him for cuts that would need stitching, though she'd been certain he had no such injuries. 'Do you need care?'

His gaze changed then into something alluring and dangerous. Into something she should run from. Into something she wanted.

'Not that kind of care, Katla.' He pushed the blankets off, revealing that he wore his breeches, and held out his hand to her. 'Join me.'

'Join you?' Shivers of cold and heat and want and need rushed through her, making her heart race and her body ache. How she yet held the lantern, she knew not. When he slid off the pallet and took it from her hand, her trembling hand, she knew it showed.

'Join me.' The lantern placed on the stool safely, he reached out and slid his hands into her hair, shaking loose the braid and letting the length of it tumble down her back. 'Join with me.'

He did nothing else then but stare into her eyes and wait. She'd never been asked before. She'd never consented before. And she could not help the tears that filled her eyes as she realised that. When he saw them, he released his hold on her head slowly and smiled, stepping back towards the pallet. She caught his hands before he let her go.

'Nay. Aye,' she said. Guiding his hands back to her head, she moved in closer. 'You surprised me.'

'My desire for you is no secret, Katla.' He took one of her hands and slid it down over his erect flesh. 'No secret at all.'

She could not help it—she stroked him through the fabric of his breeches, curving her hand around the length and width of him. As she slid from the top of it to the sac at the bottom, her fingers curled under it, feeling the weight against her palm. He hissed and, when she eased her hold, he nodded *and* shook his head.

'Aye. Nay.'

Now she smiled, also a thing she never thought would be in the midst of bed play as his words almost mirrored hers. She wanted him. She wanted him to do what he'd spoken about. She wanted to choose this. She...

Chose this.

'I have never been asked for my permission before, Brandt. I was not expecting such a thing.' She caressed him once more as she lifted her head and met his intense blue gaze. 'Aye, Brandt Sigurdsson, I will join with you.'

Katla released him then to step back. Reaching for the brooches that held up her gown, she unpinned them and let it fall. When she tugged on the ties that closed her shift, he touched her hand.

'Let me?'

His voice was hoarse then and her body recognised the sound of arousal. She dropped her hands away and waited. The sight of his large, strong hands shaking as they reached across the space between them made her feel better. She was not the only nervous one here.

'Will you be gentle with me?'

She hated the vulnerability that she could hear in those words. She hated exposing her fears to him. She hated the very weakness they showed about her. Katla wished she'd never spoken them aloud.

'Will you?' he asked, tugging the laces free and sliding the edges of the fabric down over her shoulders and arms. Her nipples tightened as the cold air touched them. Then her whole body arched as he caressed the shift down over her belly and hips until it dropped to the floor around her feet. 'Will you be gentle with me, Katla Thorfinnsdottir?'

He did not wait for her answer. He dropped to his knees before her and took the tip of her breast into his mouth. Gasping against the pleasure of it, she grabbed his shoulders for her legs would not hold her up. His tongue rubbed over the sensitive nipple, circling it again and again as pleasure filled her blood and heated every part of her. When his teeth grazed it, her body shuddered.

'Ah, you wish the other to be attended to, Katla? No worries.'

And then he did…attend to the other breast. She slid her fingers into his hair and may have grasped it, trying to hold him close as he tasted and licked. His hands caressed under and around her breasts as his mouth gave her such pleasure unlike anything she'd felt before. The place between her legs grew wet and ached for his touch. Would he touch her there, too?

As if he could read her thoughts, he laughed as he suckled her breasts. One hand slid down until it rested on her curls and just stopped, teasing her body as much as if he moved those strong fingers. The heel of his hand pressed against the mound of her and drove her mad with need. She wanted his fingers inside her.

'Soon, Katla. Soon.' She opened eyes she hadn't realised she'd shut and met his amused gaze. 'I may talk in my sleep, but you talk when you think.' He eased his way back to sit on his heels, releasing her.

At first, he did not move. His breathing sounded laboured and she could see the outline of his flesh against his breeches. The size of it, the feel of it, both scared and attracted her. Katla then realised he was just staring at her. She made to cover herself with her hands when he took them and guided them away.

'Nay. I would look on all of you.'

And he did. The fire in his eyes warmed her as it moved over her, stopping at her breasts, her belly, her hips and then lingering on the golden curls that covered her mound. How could only a gaze cause such a storm of feelings within her?

She ached. She blazed with heat and trembled with cold. Her skin felt tight and her breasts swollen. Her core needed. Her mouth…her mouth wanted to touch and taste his skin. Her tongue wanted to feel the markings on his chest to see if they had a flavour.

She…wanted it all with him.

'I think we need a pallet at your back.'

He stood and scooped her into his arms, then carried her to the pallet. Instead of climbing in next to her, he stood before her and smiled. But it wasn't a friendly one. Not even a secret one. Nay, the smile on his face spoke to her body of hunger and desire and need. Then he reached down and loosened the belt at his waist and drew it off. A tug on the laces and his breeches opened, allowing his manhood to spring free. Brandt pushed his breeches to the floor and stepped out of them, standing entirely naked before her.

Katla had seen his flesh before, when she had tended to his injuries or in those early days when he was ill. But now, full of vigour and arousal, it was something quite different. The size of it, knowing where he would put it, should have terrified her and yet, the only trembling in her body now was from desire for him. When she reached out to touch it, he backed away and shook his head.

'Too many things to do and I do not want to embarrass myself,' he whispered. She did not fully understand his words, but he gave her no chance to. Instead, he walked to the end of the pallet and knelt at her feet. With the gentlest of touches, he guided her legs apart and moved between them. 'Open for me,' he whispered. 'Let me in.'

Her knees fell open to him and she pushed up on her elbows to see what he was doing. He leaned over and kissed her legs, moving inch by inch up until he reached the inside of her thighs. Whether the sight of it or the pleasure of it was the cause, Katla lost her breath. With his hands beneath her legs, he eased her knees up and out, allowing him to see the most intimate part of her.

'By the gods, Katla, you are beautiful.'

Men were strange creatures and his words confused and aroused her. When she felt his heated breath against the sensitive folds of flesh, she almost screamed. Her body arched, trying to get closer to his mouth, and he moved in, his mouth against her flesh in a way she'd never experienced before.

Was this wrong? Was this strange? Did men do this to women? When he pressed his mouth to her and slid his tongue against her flesh, she cared not. She just felt. Felt the exquisite roughness of his tongue as it swept across her. Felt the waves of aching and need that spread to every part of her. Her mouth watered. Her skin itched and ached to be caressed. Her core shivered and tightened until she felt she might die from the pleasure. But the moment when he found some small spot of her, a tiny bit of flesh hidden within the folds that he was tasting, she did die.

From deep inside, the tremors began, alternately tightening and loosening until she was certain she fell apart in pieces. Her hips rocked against his mouth and he suckled her flesh as he had her breasts, hard and softer, faster and slower, on and on until she quaked from the power of the pleasure that filled her. She would have screamed, but no breath or sound would leave her chest or mouth.

Then, as the first bit of sense returned, Brandt eased away from that place and kissed his way up her body, sliding his hips down and his flesh to the place that still hungered and still throbbed. His mouth reached hers and she tasted the saltiness of her own essence when she opened to him.

Relentless. Breath-stealing. Hunger-building kisses. She clutched at his shoulders and slid her hands down his back, caressing him. He lifted from her mouth and met her gaze. In his, she saw an unmet need and desire. She felt the hard length of him poised between her legs.

'Join with me, Katla. Now?'

Tears trickled from the corners of her eyes as she nodded her permission. And in the next moment, he eased his way into the folds of flesh that yet throbbed from the pleasure he'd given her and he filled her with himself.

She'd expected pain. She'd suspected he would lose his control as Trygg always did. She'd thought she knew what to expect from this part. Instead he proved her wrong.

So wrong.

With a hand beneath her, he angled her hips so he could move fully inside her. The core of her tightened around his length and she felt every movement he made as he slowly thrust and then pulled back. Katla slid her legs around his and pulled him in until, with the next thrust, he almost touched the deepest part of her. With an amazing ability to tease and torment, Brandt continued until her body was wound tight and her muscles around his flesh wanted release.

'More,' she whispered against his mouth. He plunged his tongue inside, seeking hers, and then his movements in her mouth mimicked that of his hard shaft in her woman's flesh. She arched her hips, trying to meet his thrusts. 'More.'

The feeling of him laughing against her mouth was sublime and she suckled on his tongue then, enjoying the feeling of being filled with him.

'More?' he asked as he thrust slow and deep. 'Like

that?' he repeated and she gasped with each plunging movement. She was watching his face as it contorted in some painful expression. As he moved deeper inch by inch, she understood that she was watching him control the desire she saw in his eyes. She tightened the muscles within her and he sighed against her mouth.

'Like that?' she whispered back.

'Katla, I am trying to go slowly. I do not wish to hurt you.' Her heart burst in that moment at his kindness and at his consideration of her needs before his own. What man did such a thing?

'More.'

She saw the exact moment when he let go and followed the demands of his flesh. Deeper than before, he filled her and thrust harder and faster. Katla moved with him, feeling the pleasure building again as her body readied for release one more time.

His hips pushed in and then he stopped. She felt his manhood harden more and then begin to throb against her flesh within. It was enough to send her spinning out of control once more. When she could think, she felt the last of his contractions and accepted his body as he relaxed against her.

Never had a man's weight felt good before. Never had being covered and held down been pleasurable. But now, with him, she relished the size and warmth of him as he lay unmoving on her, recovering from their joining. He yet filled her and she was careful not to move because she was not willing to lose this closeness, this intimacy, between them. His head rested against her shoulder and she listened as his breathing returned to a slow, regular pace.

'My arse is cold.'

Of all the words that could be uttered in a moment like this, those were none she'd considered. Katla laughed and turned her head to find him looking at her.

'You have blankets here,' she said, grabbing hold of the one they were lying on and tugging at it.

'But I do not wish to move.' He smiled and shifted his hips just enough to let her know his flesh was still within hers.

'I am quite warm,' she teased, arching her hips slightly to make him feel it, too.

Without warning, he wrapped his arms around her and rolled on to his back, which positioned her over him now and exposed her naked body to the cold air of the cell. 'Beast,' she whispered.

Then she realised that she liked the way it felt to be straddling his hips. As the chill air covered her, her nipples grew taut and gooseflesh rose on her skin. Brandt, with a wicked smile, stroked up her arms and covered her breasts with his hands.

'I could keep you warm, Katla,' he whispered. 'I know ways.'

Her deep shiver ruined it and he laughed as he turned again, bringing her to his side and tugging the blankets over them. Their bodies separated then and Katla felt empty after the way they'd joined. They lay in silence for a while and Katla was grateful for the heat of his body. Brandt never stopped touching her, though—he stroked her back and her arm, touched his mouth to her hair and forehead and even slid his legs against or over hers.

When he cleared his throat, Katla had a feeling she was not going to like what he said. Mayhap it was the way his body tensed as he leaned back to watch her face as he spoke? She would have prepared herself, but she had no way of knowing what was coming.

'No matter what comes in these next days and weeks, I pray you know that I will treasure what just happened between us, Katla.' He leaned over and kissed her mouth so softly it made her want to weep. 'No matter what is said or done, this, what we shared, had nothing to do with your father or my fight with him.'

Stunned by his words, Katla pushed herself up to sit next to him. Reaching over, she grabbed her shift and tugged it over her head, keeping the worst of the cold off her skin.

'What would this have to do with Thorfinn?' she asked. Even as the words came out, she knew what others would say if it became known he had done this with her.

'I wanted you, Katla. That you wanted me in return and allowed me to share pleasure with you is a blessing of the gods.' She nodded in agreement, while his eyes darkened with concern. 'I did not do this to insult you or your father. Or to strike at his honour by shaming his daughter.'

Had she even thought that something like that could or would happen? Nay. She believed they'd hidden their meetings in the dark of night and no one knew. She'd heard no rumours or whispers spreading about her and Brandt, other than about her tending his wounds as ordered by Thorfinn. Alpia might suspect. Alfaran might, as well, but no one else. And if Thorfinn ordered her presence here, no one could question it anyway.

He held his hand out and she took it, allowing him to entwine their fingers and draw her closer.

'After all you have done for me, I would never harm you, Katla. I want you to know that.'

'I think you just showed me that, Brandt.' Then she knew what she must tell him. So that he knew the truth even if others made allegations or accusations against him or them. 'I have one thing to tell you. Something you should know. Well, two things,' she said, sitting down on the pallet where he still laid.

'You gave me a choice I have never had before and will not again unless we succeed. And I will treasure that for ever.' He lifted their joined hands to his mouth and kissed hers.

'And the second thing?' He turned to his side and leaned up on his arm as she took and released a breath.

'This,' she said, motioning to his pallet and his na-kedness, 'could never insult Thorfinn because I am not his daughter.'

Chapter Sixteen

Of all the things she could have said or all the ways in which she could have reacted after their joining, this was never one in his thoughts. Or in the realm of possibilities at all.

Not Thorfinn's daughter?

'Do you jest?' he asked, searching her face for some clue.

'Nay, 'tis the truth,' she said in a too-calm voice. 'I only found out recently and yet, when I think on it, it makes sense.' Not to him. Thorfinn had claimed her as such, raised her as such and called her so.

'How did you discover this?' He sat up then and released her hand. Brandt slid to the edge of the pallet, grabbed his breeches and tugged them on. Standing, he tied the laces closed. Only when he noticed the silence did he turn to see her staring at him. At his body. His body felt the heat of her gaze. Right now, he must ignore the pull he felt towards her and sort this out.

'My aunt told me. We were talking a few days ago

and I knew she was not telling me all that she knew about why my father—why Thorfinn was so different towards me now than he had been years ago.'

'And she just told you this?' He found the near-empty jug of mead and offered her some first before taking a mouthful and swallowing it. 'How has no one known before?'

Brandt thought back and could not bring a single instance to mind of when he'd heard any rumour or whisper about such a thing. As Thorfinn's friend and ally until his marriage to Kolga, his father would have heard or known about it. Men talk. Men talk freely when ale flows and Sigurd would have heard such a thing, either from his friend or in all the hours they'd spent in feasts or fighting or just in being together so often.

''Tis not something Thorfinn would want known. No matter that he is Norse and has laid claim to these lands, the people here support him because of his wife's ancestral claim to these lands and because of her daughters' continuing claims. I know that your people have shown over and over again that resisting them is futile, but here, here, we have come to this accommodation. The belief that Thorfinn honours their old ways has led to prosperity and peace.' She shrugged. ''Twould be in his own best interests not to let it be known.'

Katla retrieved her gown and dressed as he watched. They had much to discuss and yet he wished their time of intimacy was not over yet.

Their joining had been unexpected, for what prisoner, what man destined to die, would have thought to find such a woman as she here, now? From the first time since they met until this one, each encounter with Katla proved to be something new and something more and something...impressive. By turns she showed herself to be intelligent, skilled, caring, stubborn, loyal and capable of such trust even after such harsh betrayal.

Katla was the kind of woman he could love. Katla could be the woman he did love. If only...

If only he knew he would succeed. If only he could reclaim his life and his inheritance and his honour. If only they'd met in a different way or time or place than this. If only he had more to give her than their time together in this cell.

'Are you well?' she asked. Walking to him, she touched his cheek with the back of her hand. 'You do not feel feverish, but you have the strangest expression on your face.'

'I am well,' he said, covering her hand with his and keeping the gentle caress from ending. 'But I feel like my wits have flown at this news. Yet, you seem happy at this change in your circumstances.'

'I have had some time to consider this, while it is new to you.'

'This is what was vexing you some days ago. When you came here in that strange mood,' he said. This made sense. 'When you asked for my answer about helping you.'

'Aye. I confess I wanted your agreement before you learned the truth.'

'This changes everything and nothing,' he said. 'If he is not your father, then you owe him no loyalty.

Especially if he sought to use you for his gain while knowing this truth. I guess the question we need an answer to is whether he knew this truth.'

'He has known for some time.' Katla sighed and shook her head. 'I believe that Kolga discovered it somehow and told him. That is when he changed towards me. After their marriage.'

'And your marriage? He ended that for you.'

'He told me at the time that he agreed to the marriage to please her. That he would find a local husband for Gemma. He did not truly turn against me until after Trygg died. When the story of how it happened made it look as though he was directly involved in it, though none dared accuse him of it.'

'Katla, this is baffling. So you think that this leads back to my aunt then? She revealed your…parentage and he turned against you?'

'Aye. I think that is exactly what happened.'

Instead of pacing now, he watched as she used her fingers to untangle her hair. When she could not reach the farthest length of it, he stepped behind her and took the mass in his hands. He tried to keep his attention on the matter at hand, but the feel of her hair was like strands of silk against his palms and his fingers.

Ingrid had liked to have hers in a braid for sleeping and so she would sit in their bed and comb hers. Brandt would watch her do it, his body hardening with each stroke for they both knew his intention. He watched her twist her long locks until they were under control in a tight braid and then could not wait to undo it and free her hair to fall around them.

Katla's hair would fall around her in a curtain if he shook it loose now. She could straddle his hips, wearing nothing but her hair, tempting him with tantalising glimpses of her breasts and the curls that drew his eye and made his mouth water for a taste of it. He divided her hair in three pieces and twisted them, over and under, over and under, trying to gain control over his unruly desire. When he reached the end and the length of it was tamed, she turned to hand him the leather strip to tie it.

Brandt had so many ideas about the way he wanted her and the way he wanted to pleasure her. Things he wanted to do with her, to her, if they only had the time and privacy. So many ways to seek and give pleasure. He thought of other places he wanted to take her—in the forest at night, on the beach as the tide moved in, in that stream fed by the hot spring outside of Maerr.

But they had much to do here and all the dreaming and imagining in the world would not accomplish what they needed to without planning. He tied off the braid and stepped away. Where was that damned jug of mead?

'I have something to tell you, Brandt,' she said as he sat on the pallet...without mead since the jug was empty now. ''Tis the actual reason I sought you out tonight.'

'More than you told me so far?' he asked. 'I think I need more mead.' She took the empty container from his hand and smiled.

'I will bring more when I can. For now, will you sit so I can tell you this?'

He sat on the pallet and pulled her closer to him. He could not explain the action, he only knew that he wanted her nearer as she made this next revelation.

'I told my father—Thorfinn, that is—what you suspected about Alfaran.'

His immediate reaction was anger, the anger that used to define his life. Anger like his father's, ready to strike out and hurt rather than be hurt. He let out a breath and understood his need to strike out was not what was needed. He needed to save that fury for when the time came so it would give him the strength to fight those he needed to. He glanced at Katla, the woman who'd done nothing but help him, and his anger dissipated.

'Why did you tell him? Was he pressuring you for something to use against me?'

'Nay. Nothing like that at all. In a way,' she said, turning to face him, 'it was the calmest conversation I have had with him in years.'

'When did you tell him?'

'Earlier today. After he fought Alfaran and was injured.' She lifted her hand and touched her forehead along the line of her hair. 'He had a deep cut and it needed stitching. As I tended him, I brought up Alfaran to him and asked if there was some connection between you and him. Father seemed surprised by the animosity in Alfaran's actions when you two did not know each other before and I told him of your suspicion.'

She slid back and tucked her leg up under her. Touching his arm, she shook her head. 'He was surprised by it, Brandt. Truly surprised by the thought of it.'

'Katla...'

'Nay, I know his expressions, Brandt. My life has been dependent on reading his face to know when his anger was going to overflow at me these last years. And when I told him, I saw confusion and shock and suspicion, but no guilt. He was surprised that a man he thought was loyal to him might not be.'

Brandt thought on her words and he did not like where it took him. He shook his head, denying the idea before he even spoke it.

'You think he's not involved? You think he did not plan this with Kolga? Come now, Katla—' He stopped when she put her hand over his mouth. He nodded and she let it fall.

'I do not think him innocent of this, Brandt. I would not insult the memory of your father, or your wife and son! But I am left wondering how he was drawn in to marry her? Why would he? And, if what I suspect is true, if she used knowledge of my mother's infidelity to turn him against me, what does she use now to keep him from telling the truth?'

'Do you think that you are too overwrought about finding out he's not your father to consider he may be at the heart of this?' As soon as the words left his mouth, he knew his error. She startled as though he had struck her.

Though Ingrid had been a kind, soft-hearted woman ruled by her emotions, never once had Brandt seen that in Katla. Oh, she was emotional and caring, but she had a strength from within that he admired. She was practical and did what was necessary. Emotions ran high in her, but they did not control her. Instead she used them to do what she must, for those who held her loyalty.

'My apologies, Katla. I did not mean to insult you in that way.' He took her hand in his and lifted it to his mouth. 'I may not understand how or why you believe this about him, but I will listen.' He kissed her palm and held her hand against his cheek.

If his father yet lived and heard him say such a thing, Brandt would find himself on the ground—put down by his overbearing, furious father. Sigurd, King of Maerr, never admitted to being wrong even when he was. And to apologise to a woman was a sin deserving of punishment.

Brandt had learned that, though he admired many things about his father, his arrogance and belief in his own infallibility was not one of them. Ruling well meant that others respected you, respected your strength and your loyalty to them and your ability to provide for them and protect them. To rule wisely, a man, a king, did not put up with fools and was not so foolish as to underestimate another's worth.

Like that of this extraordinary woman sitting before him. He would not be stupid enough to undervalue her advice and to disregard her words. He was more certain than ever that his father's inability to take a woman seriously might have led to his death.

'The reason I came to you for help was that I know a woman alone cannot carry out her plans without help. I need your protection and aid to escape here.'

'And my aunt could not carry out any plan of vengeance against my father without the help of a man?'

'Or a number of them. This plot seems to spread over so many places I suspect she has a number of men assisting her with it. You said one of your brothers travelled to Constantinople and was still a target for an attempt to kill him?'

'Aye.'

Brandt considered her words. He'd thought the same thing himself about a lone woman succeeding, but discounted it because he had suspected Thorfinn was at the centre of it all. But, what if Thorfinn was only a spoke in Kolga's wheel of deception and revenge? What if Kolga was at its centre?

He felt as though he'd been hit over the head with an axe.

How had they missed this before? The answer was simple—they underestimated the hatred and abilities of a woman. Just as their father had when first he had slighted her by choosing her sister over her and then by laying claim to lands she believed would be hers.

And now they were in her control.

He glanced over at Katla and smiled. She'd made sense of this all when others, men, could not. Oh, she'd known that Kolga had been a bad influence on Thorfinn and his treatment of her. She'd been the one to see that there had to be a wider plan and to realise that Kolga needed connections to see it through.

'How many do you think she has in league with her?'

For too long, he'd tried to sort through his aunt's

web of lies and the help he'd needed had just come from the woman he'd started to…love. His thoughts scattered as that revelation sank in.

He loved Katla Thorfinnsdottir.

The woman who'd saved his life several times over. The woman whose father, in name and upbringing if not in truth, was his bitterest enemy. The woman who'd insulted him and taunted him and teased him.

And who'd shown him how to love again in the dark of night in this prison chamber.

He waited for the pain that should strike him at the thought of betraying Ingrid in this way. He waited for the guilt of finding love with his enemy's daughter. Even as the image of Ingrid in his thoughts disappeared and as she spoke words he could not hear, he waited for the reaction he expected.

And it did not happen.

He had rejoiced with his brothers when they found women who were worthy of their love, even in the midst of this joyless hunt for the truth. But he had never expected that he would find such a woman so close to the time of reckoning. At a time when he wanted so much to keep her and yet had nothing at all to offer her but more pain and more loss.

'Brandt?'

He blinked several times and met her gaze, seeing her somehow differently now. Seeing her as the man who loved her. The man who would protect her and help her escape. The man who would, at the end of this adventure, leave her.

'I was thinking about something else,' he said, shaking his head. 'What did you say?'

It took a few more moments before the wonderment of this new feeling eased and before he could pay heed to her words and not the way her eyes flashed like the lights in a winter sky. Before he could hear the sense in her words rather than the sounds she made when he pleasured her. Finally, he dragged his attention back to her very logical explanation of how his aunt had plotted against his father and family, even using her own sister to pay for some of the evil deeds.

By the time Katla rose to leave the cell, they had most of it sorted out. Some bits were yet missing— reasons for Thorfinn's marriage to Kolga and how much of a part he'd played—while others had been right in front of them all along. And while he did not wish to believe that Thorfinn had been involved in his father's murder, they could not explain that away…yet. If the gods favoured them, mayhap they would discover that before Brandt faced that final challenge?

He followed Katla to the door and took her in his arms before she could open it. Sliding his hands up, careful not to disturb the braid, he cupped her face and leaned down to kiss her. Looking on her now, knowing the truth within his heart, he saw not only the beauty of her face, but also her innate intelligence and kindness that had drawn him in.

He touched his mouth to hers, savouring the way she opened to him. Dipping his tongue inside her, he tasted her, trying to remember this for later when she was gone. She clung to him then and he kissed her until they both lost their breaths. When he eased back, she stared at him with questions in her gaze. As though she felt the difference in this kiss over the dozens he'd shared with her. As though she understood the message his mouth had given her.

One that he could never say in words.

'I will come back and bring more mead,' she said, reaching for the jug and turning back to the door.

'Have a care, Katla,' he warned. 'If Kolga has Alfaran here, others may also be doing her bidding. Trust no one.'

At first, she looked ready to say something else, but she nodded and left, the key turning in the lock quickly. As the sound of her footsteps grew softer and softer, Brandt held on to the opening in the door and listened, leaning his head against it. Alone, he allowed the thought to flow clearly.

He loved Katla Thorfinnsdottir.

May the gods help them all.

Chapter Seventeen

Over the next eight days and nights, winter tried to keep its grasp on the lands of Katanes and Brandt found himself inside more than outside. The nature of the storms changed though from heavy wet snow at the beginning to a frigid mix of rain, sleet and snow at the end. But the last one that battered Wik Castle and its inhabitants for two days was one of relentless rains that washed the keep, buildings and even the village and roads clear of any lingering snow.

This change was apparent to those in the keep, for everyone who knew of the patterns of winter there remarked on it. The old woman who scrubbed the floors of the storage rooms where they had him working announced that the worst of it was over. An old man who brought animals to the kitchen from the village declared the same. To a one, those living in Wik were pleased to know that spring was on its way.

To Brandt Sigurdsson it only meant that his meeting with fate moved closer. A strange awareness filled him with the passing of those days and the nights. These could be, if the gods did not favour his cause, his last days alive. He might never see his brothers or his mother again here. If he died fighting, he might find his father waiting for him in one of the gods' halls in the afterlife. He should be happy to face his destiny and try to regain the honour they'd lost.

And yet, with each passing day of labour and with each night filled with Katla's visits, he worried over the outcome. Oh, he did not fear death itself. He had faced it many, many times in battles and here not so long ago. It was leaving her alone that worried him the most. Leaving her to Kolga's cold choice of husband and knowing the brutality she would face. Seeing the fear in her expressive gaze when they loved reminded him that they must succeed in escaping.

Word made its way through the keep that Alfaran had disappeared and could not be found. Brandt told Katla that he suspected Thorfinn had rid himself of a threat and done it without a ship to be had. Though she was not convinced Thorfinn had killed the man, she did agree that the disappearance was suspicious.

So far, they'd secreted away supplies for their journey south—cheese, dried meat, skins of ale and other foods—along with extra cloaks and shoes. Katla had been sewing coins into the hems of her gowns and managed to collect another small sack so they could pay for things they needed.

Her aunt had arrived in the middle of one night, thankfully after they were dressed again, to explain about her cousin who lived in Inbhir Nis. As Alpia explained, he watched Katla's face explode in surprise at the story of her mother's cousin who'd married a Pict nobleman in the main city in the south of Alba where the river connected to the northern seas. He'd never travelled to it, but he had heard of the place and had passed close to it on his journey here.

If they could travel by ship it would take less time than by land, but it was the perfect place for Katla and her sister to seek a new life. It would take several days or more to get to the town, if the weather held and the roads south were clear. From that place, she could travel west to the islands or south into the Angles' lands or even to Eidyn in the centre of Alba on its eastern coast. Before he left her to return here, Brandt would tell her where his brothers were if she needed to seek them out for help.

Once the storms had passed and it felt as if there was a change coming in the weather they knew they must go soon. Katla remarked on the buds seen on the trees and the way animals returned from their winter burrows and Brandt knew their time was running out. Then, one morning, a messenger arrived for Thorfinn from one of his crews in the south with word that ships had been sighted on the seas and that trade would be resuming soon.

It was time.

Katla went to him earlier than ever before. Once the potion she'd made had rendered most of those within the keep asleep, they must get on their way. The biggest challenge facing her was to convince Gemma to come along.

She'd avoided speaking of any of this with her sister for fear of being overheard or for fear that Gemma would let some detail slip out and word would get back to Thorfinn. The tension among the people here since Alfaran's disappearance was growing and all Gemma would have to do to disrupt their plans was to share something.

No, she and Brandt had agreed that Gemma would be told at the last moment before they left. If need be, Katla was prepared to take the girl away even if she did not agree. Brandt's earlier suggestion to tie her to a horse might come to fruition if that was how it had to be to get her sister away to a safer life.

Carrying the cumbersome sack under her arm, she made her way down to the dungeon as soon as it was safe to do so. She would free him and then get her sister once the whole of the keep settled for the night. She'd found his sword and dagger and axe where Alfaran had stored them and carried them back to Brandt. Though they could find weapons on their way out, she thought he might like to have his own if he needed to fight anyone.

'You are making enough noise to rouse the dead,' he said as she unlocked the door. 'Here, let me...' He took the bulky bundle from her and kissed her as she passed him.

The ease with which he touched her or kissed her still surprised...and pleased her. For so long any touch had meant pain or retribution, but he'd shown her it did not have to be that way. By the gods, what she wouldn't do to have a man like this at her side!

'Is something the matter?' he asked as he placed it on the pallet and turned back to her. 'You have the strangest look in your eyes.'

Why? Why did she have to find love now? When it would be torn away from her in the name of vengeance?

'Nay, I am well,' she said, turning away to wipe the tears out of her eyes. She used her retrieval of a small bottle within her pouch to cover it. If she began crying now, she might never stop. 'Not a jug, but enough for this night?'

'Mead?' He laughed as she handed it to him. 'I hope you managed to sneak some into our supplies. I do not remember mead as good as this one.'

He pulled the cork and took a taste of it before grabbing hold of her and kissing her. The taste of him and the mead on his tongue made her melt against him. In less time than she would have guessed, the bundle was pushed aside, their garments lay in a puddled pile next to the pallet and she was suckling on his tongue.

They'd learned in previous encounters to make certain the blankets were not caught beneath them and she laughed against his mouth as he pulled them free before moving over her on the pallet. His body was big and strong and hot on hers. Katla slid her hands down from his shoulders to his back and then hips and legs, stroking as she enjoyed the feel of him. He eased his way between her legs and waited for her to meet his eyes.

'Katla?'

'Aye.' The word came out as a sigh and he entered her before she finished it.

He moved slowly, filling her with his flesh by simply moving his hips. He did not thrust or plunge, he just filled her emptiness and waited for her to pull him in. Tightening the muscles that surrounded him, she watched the pleasure show on his face. He liked that. So, she held him that way until he slid almost out of her. Her body felt empty, hollow, without his flesh there.

He did it again and, though this usually drove her mad with the need for him to do more, to move harder or faster or deeper, this night the slow pace of it seemed right to her. Katla closed her eyes then and let go of worry and thought and only felt. His heat-slick skin on hers. The hairs on his chest tickling her breasts with every move. The strength in his thighs and arms as he held himself in check and moved over her. The fullness at her core as he claimed her. So much power within him and he was so gentle with her, listening and moving as she needed and wanted him to.

This time, it happened slowly and quietly. Her body reached satisfaction on a sigh and a moan rather than the explosive release of their other joinings. As she let go to enjoy the wave of pleasure rushing through her, she felt his flesh harden and throb and then the warm rush of his release inside of her.

It felt…right.

She thanked the gods that she had this time with him before anything else happened. If their plan failed, if she was forced into marriage with Arni, she would have this in her memories for the rest of her life. Katla remained perfectly still, letting moment after moment go by without moving or speaking and barely even breathing. Anything not to break the magic that surrounded them. After a short time, she felt the rumble in his chest before she heard the laugh.

'Is your arse cold again?' she asked, watching his eyes light up with humour.

'Aye,' he said as he tugged the blanket over them.

He rolled them, turning on to his side and trapping her with a leg over hers to keep her close. Though he slipped out of her, she could feel his flesh against her as they lay facing each other.

'Katla—'

'Brandt—'

They laughed together and then quieted. She waited for him, but he nodded for her to speak first. The words tangled in her throat, for what she wanted to say to him was not fair. But it was in her heart and she would regret never saying it to him when they did finally part.

'I have fallen in love with you, Brandt. These weeks and days have given me something I never thought possible for me. And I will treasure our time and the care you have shown me for the rest of my days,' she said.

'Katla—' She pressed her fingers to his lips to stop him. If he spoke she would lose her courage.

'Would you…could you…do you think…?'

She paused, losing her nerve and the words she wanted to say to him. The request she wanted to make of him. Until he leaned across the space between them and kissed her. He touched her mouth so softly, she began to cry.

'If you did not have to die, Brandt…if you could find it in you to give up your vengeance, would you?' Tears streamed down now, for she knew it was not fair to ask such a thing of him. Yet the love in her heart pushed her to try to save him. 'You could come with me on the morrow. Not just to escort me and to return, but to stay. We could go to Inbhir Nis or go to one of your brothers. They have found new lives. Surely they would not begrudge you the same?'

She kissed him now and knew that the taste of desperation filled her mouth. She knew she should not have asked a man who lived by his honour to disregard it, yet her love for him made her want him to know he had another choice. When she drew away, he rubbed the tears off her cheeks and shook his head.

'Do not answer now, Brandt. Just think about it. Think of the possibilities if you tried to live instead of trying to die.'

He took her fingers and kissed them one by one, tugging her hand away then. She wanted to close her eyes and not see him as he refused her.

'Katla, my love,' he whispered, filling her with hope for a brief, shining moment. 'You have given me more than I thought possible. You taught me to live when I wanted to die. You taught me to love when I thought that was meant for others. I will remember every time you trusted me to touch you, to love you.'

He kissed her then even as she cried. Then he gathered her in his embrace and she listened to his heart beat against her ear. Brandt smoothed her hair out of her face and just held her. Katla.

'If I could give up my quest for vengeance, nay, to reclaim the honour of my family, for anyone, it would be for you. If I could walk away and find another life with anyone, it would be with you.'

'Brandt, don't. Please do not...' She knew she would have to live with his refusal, but she did not wish to hear it now. 'Give me now. Your choice can wait until the morrow.'

They loved once more—this time it was about possession and claiming. Now that he'd spoken of love, she wanted all of him. She wanted nothing held back and she gave him everything she had within her. If the last time had been gentle, this was ferocious as though they were each trying to absorb the other. When, at last, they lay spent and exhausted in each other's arms, Katla understood that this was farewell.

They dressed in silence, neither of them looking at the other. When they were ready, Brandt opened the bundle and lifted his sword out, holding it before him. For the blink of an eye, sorrow filled him as he looked upon it and then resolve filled his face and she knew he would never be hers again.

'My thanks for finding these,' he said. 'A battle is always better when you know the weapons in your hands.' He unbuckled his belt and slid the scabbard on to it, positioning the sword where he was most comfortable. The axe slid into a loop on his other side and the daggers into a small leather holder on the cross garters around his legs.

'Meet me at the small storage shed before the gate. That is where our supplies are stored.'

'You do not wish help with your sister?' he asked, resting his hand on the hilt of his sword. Somehow, he looked taller now and more formidable than the man to whom she had just given her love.

'Nay. I will see to her and meet you at the shed. Have a care going into the yard. The guards circle the walls and they may not yet be affected by the ale.' She turned to go, but he took her by the arms and stood before her.

'Katla, if you escape and run into any trouble, my brother Danr serves King Knut on Skíð. Seek him there if you need his help.' Stunned that he trusted her to know about one of his brothers, she just nodded. 'And Rurik is now Lord of Glannoventa in Northumbria. Sandulf lives in Strathclyde and Alarr is in Éireann, where he is kin to the King. If you need anything, send to them and they will help.'

She nodded, speechless that he'd given her so much knowledge about his brothers. He had not trusted her for a long time, yet now it warmed her breaking heart.

'I will,' she whispered.

'Go now,' he said as he released his hold on her. ''Tis time.'

Katla handed him the key to the cell and made her way back to her chamber to change into something better for travelling. Then she must get her sister and speak to her aunt. And then, pray that the gods would look favourably on their plan and protect them all.

So she was surprised when she opened her chamber door to find Gemma sitting on her bed. As she closed the door, trying to think of what to say, she spied her aunt sitting on a chair in the corner.

'Gemma, Aunt, I did not expect to find you here,' she said. She gave a questioning glance at her aunt.

'I have been talking with Gemma and she is ready to go with you,' her aunt said.

Surprised by that statement, she looked at her sister who returned her stare with one of her own. For a moment, she did not look like a young girl. She looked older than her years.

'I know you think me a child, Katla, but I am not one. Aunt Alpia answered the questions you would not.' Looking at Gemma, Katla could see the tears glistening in her eyes then. 'I do not want you harmed. I do not want you to suffer because you protect me.'

Katla opened her arms and Gemma flew into them. 'Gemma. I promised our mother I would do anything to protect you. And I will.'

'I know you have shielded me from Father's worst and I do not know what I would do without you.'

'The sad thing is,' Aunt Alpia said, drawing their attention, 'if Thorfinn honours his promise to fight Brandt to clear his father's name and Thorfinn loses, I do not know what will happen to these lands and to you two.'

Katla had not thought of that possibility at all. She had been so grieved at the thought of Brandt either not being allowed to challenge or that he would die in the fight that the very real chance that Thorfinn would lose, and lose everything, had not occurred to her.

'If he fights Brandt and loses, it will mean his death. Even if he does not die in the fight, the King will execute him at that very moment. Without any further

appeal. His lands will be forfeit and the King may...
the King will take control of Wik and the lands passed
through your mother. I fear you two will suffer for
that as well.'

'So, it is best that we leave now?' Gemma asked.

'Aye. No matter what happens, if you are here when
Kolga arrives, your lives will not be as you want them
to be.'

'Aunt, you should come with us,' Katla urged. 'You
will not be safe.'

'If the time comes, I will find a way to seek refuge elsewhere, Katla. I have lived this long, through
turmoil and upheaval, and I can survive a little longer to help you both escape.' She looked at Gemma.
'You need a heavier cloak than that. Fetch it from your
chamber quickly now, Gemma.' When her sister left,
Alpia faced her. 'I think your father, Thorfinn, knows
you are planning something.'

'Then why would you tell us to go? Alpia, if he
does, why is he not stopping us?' Katla's thoughts were
thrown into confusion. Did he know? Would he stop
them? Even now, had he or his men intercepted Brandt?

'Child,' she said, taking Katla's trembling hands in
her own calm ones, 'I think he knows Brandt is right.
I think he knows that if Brandt stays here now, Kolga
and her minions will kill him and never give him a
chance to speak before the King.'

'I have not understood why Father—why Thorfinn
even allowed him to live at all.'

'A guilty conscience mayhap? With no honourable
way out now that he is too far involved?' Alpia offered

those choices and yet Katla could not believe either was true. Thorfinn did his own bidding and made his own choices.

Yet, at other times since Brandt's arrival, it did appear he had taken steps to ensure the man survived. Even when Alfaran disobeyed his orders, Thorfinn interceded not once, but twice to stop him. And he gave Brandt more food than any prisoner could expect. And the chance to labour and build his strength. Why had she never considered that before?

Gemma arrived back at her door and Alpia followed them to the steps. She hugged her aunt as did Gemma and Alpia sent them on their way with words of caution and hope. Katla pulled Gemma in close as they made their way through the corridor and along the edge of the hall, where many had fallen asleep as they were at table. Some lay on the floors. The sound of snoring echoed around them as she hurried her sister along.

Soon, they were in the yard, staying in the shadows as they approached the storage shed where Brandt should be waiting for them. When the guards above shifted their positions, Katla led Gemma inside. She could not help the smile on her face when she saw him.

'Gemma, you can carry that small sack.' She pointed at one her sister could manage as she picked up a heavier one. Brandt gathered the rest and they waited for a safe time to leave the shelter of the shed. 'I will take you to a gate, hidden near the back wall, that opens to a path along the water's edge. Pray that the horses I arranged are waiting just outside the village.'

'I need to stop and find my supplies, too,' Brandt said softly.

'I thought you brought only your weapons and cloak.'

He smiled and shook his head. 'Nay. I left some personal things hidden away for when I could get them.'

'You were very certain of yourself,' Gemma said to him, narrowing her gaze and studying him as though she'd not seen him before. 'Are all Norsemen arrogant like you?'

'Gemma!'

Brandt only let a low laugh out, but his smile showed that he was enjoying Gemma's dry wit and attitude.

'Aye, my lady. We are all arrogant, but many are even more so than I.'

Gemma's reply, a little huff, did give Katla pause. The sound did not show dismissal of the idea—indeed, the sound made Katla worry that Gemma would find this purported arrogance appealing.

'Now,' Brandt whispered with a nod. 'Go and I will follow.'

Katla led them to the hidden gate and out, along the shoreline up to the road some distance away. Horses stood waiting for them as promised and Katla offered up silent thanks to Alpia for all her help. Once mounted, they rode south, keeping to the edge of the road so they would not be seen.

Katla turned back to look just before the bend in the road that would lead them away from the only true home she'd ever had. The guards were not on top of the walls now, her potion having taken effect, yet she could see a man. One man.

From this distance she could not identify him, but mad as it seemed, she thought it was Thorfinn watching them ride away. He never moved from the spot and he was still there when the curve of the road took them out of the line of sight.

Could it have been him? Did he know of their plans as Alpia suspected? Would he have let them go if he did?

'Katla, have a care,' Brandt said just loud enough for her to hear him. She turned to him and the road ahead.

The escape was underway and all they could do was try. If Thorfinn knew, it was too late now for her to worry over it.

May the gods above and below protect their endeavours!

Chapter Eighteen

Exhaustion set in as quickly as did the cold as they made their escape in the middle of the night. He wanted them miles from Wik before they stopped.

Brandt had kept his attention up and watched and waited for Thorfinn's men to give chase, yet no one had followed them. Not in the first hour nor in the ten or twelve since they'd left Wik Castle. Katla's preparations had been done well—foodstuffs, ale, even additional cloaks—all packed efficiently and ready to go. They'd found horses where she expected them to be and Brandt enjoyed the feel of being out and away.

He knew this was only a temporary sojourn for him, only until he saw Katla and Gemma on their way south, and then he would return to Thorfinn and the rest. He decided that he would enjoy this small bit of freedom. Gemma, as it turned out, was a good traveller, never complaining, doing as she was asked and following instructions well.

Katla seemed restless and unsettled as they made

their way south. He could not say it was nervousness or worry over being discovered. Or even uncertainty over the choice she'd made. Nay, the strange mood began just after they'd left and after he'd observed her staring back at the castle just before they rode out of sight of it.

When he had asked her about it later, she brushed off his questions and rode in silence. He tried to reconcile himself to the growing distance between them. Last night, the time spent in her arms, was their farewell. Mayhap it was easier for her to make this break more definite? And as they crossed the miles towards Inbhir Nis, the distance and the silence between them grew. And he did not like it at all.

With nothing else to say, nothing he could offer her to change things between them, he did not fight it, spending most of his time speaking to her sister when they could. The girl reminded him of the years watching his younger brothers grow into manhood, for she had opinions about everything with little or no experience in life upon which to base them.

Yet, when she did speak of Katla, her voice filled with an honesty that revealed she'd seen and heard and knew much, much more than even Katla guessed. Gemma might be innocent, but she was not stupid.

Shortly after dawn broke, Brandt knew they needed to rest. Riding ahead, he searched for a good location— one protected from view from the road, one where they could sleep unaccosted and unseen. When Katla and Gemma reached him, he guided them back to it and they set up a small camp.

'After we eat, we should try to get some sleep. We will travel through much of this night if possible.' A groan from Katla made him smile for she, rather than the girl, was more open in her discomfort. 'Katla, you and I can take turns keeping watch. I will go first. Settle where the ground is mostly dry and I will wake you later.'

She did not argue with him, she simply gathered their sacks and supplies together, used their extra cloaks and blankets for protection and pulled Gemma close to sleep. In a way, he would rather have had an argument of some kind with her. At least then he would have seen the spirit he knew was within her displayed once more. All he saw was sadness in her gaze.

In that moment, he wanted to tell her he would stay with her. He wanted a new life with her in the centre of it. He wanted to have her to wife. They could live with one of his brothers. Rurik, now lord over lands in Northumbria, would take them in and Brandt could fight for him.

He wanted…he wished…he…

Could not.

So, words that would beg her to be his for always remained stuck in his throat, making it difficult to even breathe and, worse, to look upon her sadness. The only thing that kept him standing was that he neither felt nor saw any recrimination in that sadness for choosing his path alone over theirs together. Somehow, though, it made him feel worse about giving her up.

He watched them taking their ease and then went back to a place closer to the road where he could see anyone travelling on it. Even though the weather had improved these last days, he did not expect many to be on the roads yet. Travel would not truly increase here in the north for some time.

In the hours they slept, Brandt considered the choice he'd made. In the heat of the massacre and its aftermath, each of them—even the gravely wounded Alarr—had sworn to discover the truth and avenge their father's death. And, year by year, they had each played their part in finding the truth. And each had found their own happiness from which he could not tear them to aid him in this final step.

He knew that they had found the same happiness with Breanne and Ceanna and Sissa and Annis that he had found unexpectedly with Ingrid in his marriage. What played on him now was the knowledge that he had been blessed by the gods with another chance at happiness with Katla. He would throw that away, throw that gift in the gods' faces, by continuing to seek his own revenge. Mayhap that was not in their plan after all?

For the first time since setting his feet on this path, Brandt doubted his choice. Doubted his resolve. Doubted his word. Had the years of exile and hardship, of loss and loneliness burned the need out of it? Had seeing what his brothers had found planted the doubt?

Nay, it had been Katla.

The gods had placed her there for him, of that he had no doubt. Her plea to him to stay and make a new life was not what he had wanted to hear, but it was what he thought the gods wanted for him, for them. Why else would their escape have been so easy? Why would Thorfinn allow it?

He staggered for a moment at the importance of this revelation—was he as senseless as she proclaimed him to be? If he left her behind, if he did not accept the gift that she was, the life she offered, aye, he was senseless and worse.

Brandt knew what he must do. He knew what his answer to her must now be. He needed to accept what she'd offered and make the best of the life the gods had granted him. He strode over to where she slept and whispered her name.

'I would speak with you.' At her puzzled expression, he held out his hand to help her to her feet. He did not speak until they were some distance from Gemma. Then, as he stared into her eyes, he admitted the truth to her.

'For all my life, rage and anger have served me well. My father expected that as his firstborn I would follow his ways and that was how he dealt with everything and everyone. I learned it at his feet and I learned it well.' He paused before saying more just to drink in the way she met his gaze and the love he saw in her eyes.

'I survived on that anger for more than three years since watching my family be torn apart. Each step of the way, the fury fuelled my life and my path. Until you, Katla. Until I saw you on the wall watching me fight your father.'

She startled at his words. 'You saw me?'

'Aye, with your bright eyes on me, how could I not?'

He smiled then, for he had remembered seeing her. Not at the time it happened, but much later. 'And then you stormed into my cell and reclaimed my life from the land of the damned. How could I defy your call?' He leaned over and pulled her closer, kissing her mouth. She did not resist him; she never did refuse him anything he asked.

'You made me think of things better ignored when I was certain of my path. I needed to seek justice for my family—it kept me alive through the worst moments in my life. Until you did that. Until you forced me to stop trying to die and to try to live.'

'Brandt, you do not have to do this,' she whispered to him.

'Ah, but I do, Katla. I have realised that the gods interfered in my plan and put you in my path. I would be the senseless, stupid creature you have called me if I ignore their gift.' He saw the exact instant that she allowed herself to hope and he relished it. 'If you will have me, that is. I cannot promise not to vex you, but I will promise to love you.'

She threw herself into his arms and he kissed her, finally accepting the love she brought to him. The love that would make him whole again and give him, give them, a life ahead of them and not behind. He would have caressed her if a voice had not interrupted.

'At least you are not as stupid as I thought,' Gemma said across the clearing. 'Arrogant to wait this long, but not stupid.'

Brandt laughed then, feeling a new hope within him.

He kissed her once more before releasing her. 'We have much to discuss, but first we must get farther south.'

'First, you must get some rest, for I cannot catch you if you fall from your horse on the road.' Although the exhaustion had left him in the face of this discovery, Brandt knew she was right. 'Come, sit here with me,' she said as she climbed into the nest of blankets and cloaks. Gemma just watched them, observing every word and action, without speaking for now.

They sat close, Katla's body soft against his side and her breath warm against his chest. Soon, the alertness eased within him and he felt the pull of sleep. How long he had dosed before she spoke his name, he knew not. But the alarm in her voice, even as she whispered, brought him awake immediately.

'Brandt, someone is coming.'

He both heard the sound of approaching horses and carts and felt them rumble in the ground under him. He waved Gemma to lie lower and he crept towards the road, keeping behind trees to cover his presence. Brandt felt Katla at his back and kept her behind him as they made their way closer.

A large group of men on horses and others in carts following them moved along the road, heading northwards. Not only men, for a woman rode in their midst, a huge man at her side. He had not seen her for nigh on three years and infrequently before that, but it took him no time at all to recognise Kolga Olafsdottir—his aunt. A gasp from Katla told him that she saw her as well.

'Who is the man at her side?' he whispered over his shoulder. But Katla had turned away and he felt her whole body begin to tremble. Turning, he found her shaking her head and staring off towards Gemma. He grasped her shoulders and turned her back to him. 'Katla, who is that man?' From her reaction, he knew even as she said the words.

'That is Arni Gardarsson,' she said in a weak voice. 'My betrothed.' Brandt stared at the hulk of a man riding at his aunt's side and noticed several things at once.

Arni must be high in her favour, for she spoke to him amicably and even touched his arm as they rode side by side.

His aunt watched Arni with intense interest and smiled at whatever he said. He did not remember her ever smiling like that before.

There was more to his aunt and Arni's relationship than a noblewoman and the commander of her guards.

The last thing he realised was the worst—he had not met this Arni Gardarsson before, but he had seen him. On that fateful autumn day of his brother Alarr's wedding feast in Maerr. For it was Arni he had seen sneaking away from the village and directing a man to Thorfinn's ship. The man who would later try to kill Sandulf.

The man who had killed their father.

Arni Gardarsson was the link between his aunt's plan and those who carried it out for her so successfully. This was the man who did what she could not.

'He is the connection, Katla. He did what she could not do.'

As he uttered those words, the truth of it sank in. They remained silent for a time after the whole retinue had passed them. So many things were swirling in his thoughts that he could not seem to pay heed to just one at a time.

Arni Gardarsson and his aunt.

Katla's terror.

His aunt betrothing the man to Katla—a reward? A payment for further silence and co-operation?

Arni Gardarsson had helped his aunt carry out her plot.

Had Thorfinn known after all? Had he been pulling the strings all along or was he just a puppet?

Arni and his aunt?

Once he thought it safe to move, he gathered Katla in his arms and carried her back to where Gemma waited, wide-eyed and scared. She took Katla's hand in hers and rubbed it, whispering soothing words that did not soothe. Indeed, she seemed more caught in terror's grip now than when they had seen the group pass them by.

Searching one of the bags, he found the bottle he wanted and held it to her mouth, pouring some in when she opened. It took a few mouthfuls before she calmed a bit. And a little more time before she was able to meet his gaze.

'He is here for me.'

'Aye, he is here. My aunt is here. But you are mine,' he said. Though his choice was made, the thought of claiming his vengeance had not simply disappeared. Even now, it made him question his decision. 'He will never have you, Katla.'

'Do you swear?' Gemma asked. She would be a

fierce warrior when grown. Fiercely loyal. Fiercely protective. Fiercely dangerous if crossed. And she'd learned it by watching her sister. He hesitated for a moment, knowing what breaking another oath would mean to him. She narrowed her gaze and asked again, 'Do you swear?'

Did this child see him wavering? Did she see the doubt in him even now?

'I will protect Katla from that man. He will never have her.' Her eyes widened and he knew she was not fooled.

A sound echoed around them then, something soft carried by the wind that swirled among the bare trees of winter. If it sounded like a god's laughter, it would serve Brandt right.

'Brandt?' Katla's voiced pierced his confusion once and for all.

'Aye, love?'

'Have you changed your mind after all?'

He looked at her, pausing to bask in the warmth of the love in her gaze, and then he answered, 'Nay, my love. I have not.'

Relief eased through her, for she had doubted his resolve once he had made the connection between his aunt and her betrothed. He had sought the truth for so long and, just when he had given up the hunt, it presented itself to him. Relief was replaced with sadness, for him, for his family, his brothers, his wife and child.

'I do not think it safe to take to the roads yet. Stragglers and latecomers may yet follow their group.'

'Where did they come from, Brandt? Why did they not land at Wik's harbour?'

''Tis possible that the recent storms blew them farther south? Once the seas are settled, they can sail the ship to Wik. But it seems my aunt could not wait on the seas.'

'Do you think she knows about you?'

'From the way she rode by, she looked neither worried nor hurried over anything. So, nay, I do not think she knows.'

'So Alfaran?' She suspected she knew, but asked him anyway.

'Is dead in a ditch somewhere. Or at the bottom of the bay tied to a boulder. I do not think your father let him live once he suspected the truth of it.'

Katla rubbed her hand over her eyes and shook her head then. Trying to keep her voice low so Gemma would not hear any gruesome details or suspicions, she whispered to him, 'But if he killed Alfaran, does that mean he is against her now?' When he did not answer quickly, she turned so she could look on him as they talked. 'I saw him watching from the wall, Brandt. I know it was him. He let us leave.'

Brandt sat up, disbelief covered his face then. 'He what? You saw Thorfinn as we left Wik?' She nodded. 'Why did you not say?' He was searching her face before she replied. 'Ah, that is what had you staring behind you for so long.'

'At first that, aye,' she said. 'Then I realised that I would never see my home again. Never visit my mother's grave or see my aunt. All my happy memories are there, Brandt.' She drew in a hitching breath. 'When I went north for my marriage, it was with the promise that I would return and inherit my mother's legacy. A lie, I know, but I believed it then.'

'And you did return,' he added.

'But now, this is for the rest of my life. Wherever I end up, in Inbhir Nis or some other place, I can never go home again if I want to live.' She wiped roughly to clear the tears away, knowing how foolish this display of emotions was in the face of the dangers they had around them. 'It is for the best. Gemma will be safe. I will be safe, we all will be safe, once we're away from here, away from them.' She nodded towards the road and the people who'd passed by.

It was the shock of seeing Arni that had thrown her into turmoil, she understood that. And, at first, the way Gemma demanded an answer from him had made her worry over his newly made commitment. When they'd talked last night, when she'd asked him to go with her, his answer had been clear in every emotion that crossed his face and in every gesture he made.

Then, something had changed his mind earlier. Something had made him accept her offer and decide to set up a new life, as his brothers had. And he'd done that without realising that the answer to his quest, the missing connection between the plan and the execution of it, would come riding down the road to him.

Part of her wanted to beg him not to change his mind. Not to go back to face his own likely destruction, for Kolga and Arni had shown how devious and dangerous they were together. Brandt facing them, even with the possible help of Thorfinn, gave her no comfort. For she had seen Arni fight many times and she'd learned two things: he did not fight fair and he did not lose. Though Brandt had recovered some of his strength, if truth be told, she was not certain he could beat the man.

Instead, she remained quiet, allowing his warmth to comfort her while she sought the right way of this. She knew his intense need to avenge his father would not be satisfied if he did not grasp it when it was so close. He would honour his word to her and Gemma, but it would eat at him. He would have failed what he'd promised his brothers—brothers he would see often if their plan included living near them.

Each and every day, the dissatisfaction would seep in, destroying the love they had until he became the angry, thwarted man his father had been.

And she would be to blame for it.

They did manage to sleep a few hours and the sun was dropping in the western sky when they took to the road once more. When she noticed him glancing back, much as she had as they'd left Wik, she knew she was losing him more with every mile they crossed.

Chapter Nineteen

They stopped hours later, after carefully avoiding the harbour where Kolga had arrived. Kolga would not have expected trouble and so only the barest of crews remained behind to watch over the ship until it could sail north to Wik. Some miles down the road, Brandt found a secluded clearing where he managed to build a small fire. At least they had heat.

The silence between them had grown and Gemma was the mediator, speaking across the growing divide to each of them. Brandt was, no matter his regrets, pleasant to her sister, engaging her in conversation and regaling her with stories of the misdeeds of his brothers. Gemma was entertained by the stories while Katla heard the sadness beneath each one. She waited for Gemma to sleep before motioning Brandt to follow her to where they'd hobbled the horses.

'I need you to do something for me,' she said. He took her in his arms and held her close. She lifted her face to watch his.

'What is that, my love?' Her heart raced at his endearment.

'I need you to go to Wik and kill Arni Gardarsson for me.'

He laughed at first, but it took no time for him to realise she was serious. 'Katla, I have made up my mind on this. I will go south with you and build a new life. See my brothers.'

'Aye, you will. We will. But first you need to do what you came here to do, especially now that you know his part in this and how it worked.' She stepped away, but he would not release her. 'Gemma and I will continue to Inbhir Nis and wait for your return.'

He said nothing. He stared at her so intensely she had to look away.

'We have another two days at most on the road?' He nodded. 'You have shown us how to do this, travel by night, sleep by day. Find a secluded place off the road. Gemma and I will do this together.'

'I would not dare to tell you that you could not do whatever you set your mind to do, Katla. But I want...'

She covered his mouth with her hands to stop him.

'I saved your life so you could do this. I did not know the details or how entwined our fates were at the time, but the gods did. They gave you the strength to live, Brandt. They gave you this chance to seek justice. I pray you take it. I pray you go back and do this. For you and for me.'

He kissed her then, taking her breath and her soul and her love as he consumed her. As though he would never kiss her again. He'd made his decision and she was both elated and devastated by it.

'I will return for you,' he said. His voice was filled with the promise he made.

'You must. I will wait in Inbhir Nis until summer, then I will seek out Danr on Skíð and wait there.'

'It should not take that long.' He studied her, his gaze making its way from her head to her toes before coming to her face again. 'Katla, if—' He stopped then and she could not tell what he'd meant to say. He began again, sliding his hand up, over her cloak until it rested…on her belly.

'If there is a baby, do not wait until summer. Go to Danr immediately.'

Katla nodded. She'd not thought about that possibility. She'd not conceived a child by Trygg and had not worried about it with Brandt. Probably foolish of her, but with so many other worries and concerns to deal with, it had not been one of them. For a long moment, she prayed for Freya's blessing in this—that she might truly have a son of Brandt's if…if he…

'I can take care of a baby, if there is one.'

He stepped back and reached inside his tunic. He held out a necklace before her, one she'd not seen before. It was shaped like the god Thor's hammer, but was in two pieces. He untied the string on which the pendant slid and then reached out to tie it around her neck.

'Show that to Danr. He knows it's mine and that I would never give it lightly to anyone. He will give you his protection. You and Gemma.'

'This is not farewell, Brandt,' she said, forcing her

voice to be steady when she truly wanted to weep. 'You will come to meet us. Go, kill Arni at the least. See what your aunt does when her minion no longer lives to carry out her orders.'

Brandt leaned in once and touched his mouth to hers.

'Have a care along the way until I see you again.'

She watched as he readied his horse, gathered the weapons he needed and mounted up. She smiled—or rather tried to smile as she watched him ride out to the road and, after one backward glance, head north.

Katla prayed once more to Freya to protect her love and to protect the baby she might have within her. When they reached Inbhir Nis she would find a way to offer a suitable sacrifice so the goddess looked favourably on her. As she settled back at Gemma's side, she reached up and touched the necklace he'd given her. Her prayers went on for some time, the last one beseeching Thor to protect the warrior on his quest.

As she finally found her way to sleep, Katla heard words whispered over and over in her thoughts. She thought at first Gemma was speaking to her, but each glance showed the girl was deeply asleep. It took a while before she understood she was hearing a memory. A young woman had come to her for help. She needed herbs, a potion, to help her.

'I need to take care of this, lady,' the girl had said. The way she covered her belly, Katla knew her meaning. Though nothing showed yet, she wanted to end it before anyone knew. 'I must…'

It was not something she did often or even liked to

prepare, but the fear in the girl's gaze spoke of desperation and need. So, mixing together the necessary herbs and liquids, she gave a small bottle to the girl with instructions. Only a few drops each day would bring on her bleeding. A few drops only.

She looked for the girl soon after that, to make certain she was well and found her—she was Kolga's maidservant—giving the bottle to Kolga and repeating the instructions to her lady.

Katla was wide awake now, seeking more of that memory from almost five years ago, from the time when Kolga first married Thorfinn. As she went over and over it in her thoughts, she realised that Kolga got very sick after that and Katla suddenly understood that connection.

Kolga had been pregnant when she married Thorfinn and had ended it shortly after their marriage. Why would she do such a thing? Her father needed and wanted an heir and their mother had passed away not long before that.

Was that the reason behind the marriage? Had Kolga's baby been his and, once the marriage was accomplished, she ended the pregnancy?

The whole matter bothered her for hours and when Gemma woke, Katla knew what she must do. She could not only pray that Brandt succeeded, she must be certain he did.

Brandt made his way north and arrived not long after Kolga and the others did. He wore his cloak to cover him and blended in with the flow of travellers arriving at Wik Castle. He moved around the carts being unloaded of their supplies, avoiding speaking or looking directly at anyone as he headed for the door and into the hall. Taking up a place near an alcove in the shadows, he watched and waited as Kolga, Arni, Thorfinn and others gathered at the table to eat supper.

From the way Thorfinn behaved, he was not happy that she had returned so soon and he even allowed Alpia to sit between them. Alpia looked ready to poison Kolga's cup; he could feel the hatred even from his distant place. Others noticed and the silence grew even as the meal progressed. Brandt moved closer, seeking a spot nearer the table and the hearth so he could hear their words better. When Kolga asked for Katla to be summoned, Brandt knew it was time.

'She is not here, Kolga. I sent her away,' Thorfinn claimed. He watched as his aunt's face flushed and the anger brought out the sharp lines of it.

'Sent her away? Surely not? She is betrothed by your own agreement to Arni. Or have you forgotten that, Thorfinn?' A simple question made ominous by her tone. A clear threat made before all was a sign that discord was at the heart of this new marriage.

'I have come to take my bride home since we can sail once more,' Arni said. He drank the cup of ale down in one swallow and banged it on the table for more. 'I have waited long enough for her.' He would have to wait much, much longer, Brandt feared.

'I am her father,' Thorfinn said, daring anyone to naysay him aloud and staring down Kolga as he spoke now. 'I decided the wedding will wait.'

'Thorfinn, this was decided before the winter. My man wishes this alliance and he wants your daughter as his bride.'

'Arni is not worthy of my daughter, Kolga. I have changed my mind.'

Kolga stood then, knocking her chair back and over, looking from one end of the hall to the other. 'Where is she, Thorfinn? I demand you bring her here now, or—'

'Or what, Wife?' Thorfinn stood then and Alpia scrambled out of the way, seeking refuge away from the table.

Kolga swore loudly and then lowered her voice to a furious whisper Brandt could not hear. But Thorfinn did and he nodded at his wife. This was not the same woman who spoke so congenially to Arni as they rode here. The woman who gave him soft smiles and touches. This was the woman he knew from his younger years—a bitter, angry, dangerous woman who would seek vengeance on the man who took from her and cast her aside. When Thorfinn shook his head, Kolga screamed out in fury.

Brandt realised that Kolga and his father Sigurd were made the same, both filled with arrogance and fury and no sense of control when they were threatened or disobeyed.

'Where is she, Thorfinn?'

'Somewhere you cannot find or harm her,' Brandt called out as he stepped from the shadows. A gasp filled the hall as everyone looked at him. He threw off his cloak and drew his sword, ever advancing to-

wards the table. Guards came running, but, unbeliev-
ably, Thorfinn waved them off.

'Why have you returned?' Thorfinn asked.

'Returned? Brandt was here? Why is he still alive?
He is an outlaw, Thorfinn. Order him killed.' The coldness in her voice shocked him. When Thorfinn did
not so order, Kolga motioned to Arni to carry out her
command.

'Killed so the truth cannot be revealed after all,
Aunt?' he asked, swinging his sword and feeling the
balance of it in his grip.

'Truth? What do you know about the truth, Brandt?'
she asked, waving to Arni who moved towards him
now. He must not be distracted by her words and instead focus on the huge warrior before him. 'Your father stole everything from me. My birthright. My place.
My lands. Then, when he betrayed the King, they were
returned to me.'

'To your son, Kolga. Not to you,' Thorfinn said.

'I know that you threatened my mother, your sister, until she paid you with the pieces of jewellery my
father gave her.' He turned then so that he remained
facing Arni in his approach. Thorfinn, it seemed, was
more ally than foe, just as Katla had tried to convince
him. 'Then you gave them to Arni to pay the assassins you hired to carry out your revenge on my family.'

The colour drained from her face for but a moment
then and a flash of true fear sparked in her eyes. 'You
cannot prove that. Thorfinn, take him away or I will—'

'You will do what, Kolga? Tell my people that Katla,
her mother's eldest daughter, is not mine?' Thorfinn

crossed his arms over his chest then. 'Will you try to incite them to rise up against me?'

Thorfinn's revelation did not have the effect Brandt thought it would, for those listening and watching barely reacted to his words. Alpia met his gaze then and smiled. She had some part to play in that, Brandt was certain.

'You managed to sow discord and mistrust in those months after the massacre. Alarr discovered that the King of Éireann played no part except that his sister was Rurik and Danr's mother who you made certain my mother hated.'

'She was a whore and deserved to be treated as such,' Kolga called out.

'He also discovered that your assassins came from Northumbria and Rurik found proof linking you to them, after he killed one of them.'

'You make no sense,' she said. 'I did none of those things. I have never been to Northumbria.'

'Ah, but your man Arni has. And he was in the village the night of the massacre, when you encouraged my brother Sandulf to leave rather than face my wrath.'

'You nearly choked him. I saved his life.'

'You put him on the same ship that the assassin Rangr was on with instructions to kill him on the way to Constantinople.'

'That was Thorfinn's ship,' she argued. 'I do not command his ships. He does.' She looked very satisfied to draw Thorfinn into the centre of it.

'Rangr fell overboard and died,' Thorfinn said

calmly, almost proudly. 'As did Trygg. And Alfaran *fell* from the wall.'

Brandt wanted to laugh, but this was deadly serious.

'Sandulf and Danr found the rest and my mother confessed her affair with Joarr was what you held over her head to make your demands. All the proof, all the lies and the killers, everything leads back to you, Kolga.'

Now his aunt looked very worried. And dangerous creatures grow even more deadly when threatened. She nodded and Brandt lifted his sword as Arni attacked.

Gods, but the man was strong! He was almost half a head taller than Brandt. And he was at the height of his fighting skills. And on and on, Brandt thought as he fought back. But Brandt not only fought for his father and his wife and son, he also fought to protect Katla, the woman he loved.

He let go of everything else in his thoughts except her. The hall faded from his view, the silence surrounded him with only the sound of clashing swords breaking through. His attention targeted the man he knew responsible for so much of the death and destruction. When Kolga called out a warning to Arni and broke the man's concentration, Brandt took advantage of it, battering him with strike after strike of his blade until he lost his balance. As Arni shifted to regain it, Brandt slashed out at his legs and cut him from behind, just as Alarr had been wounded.

The man fell to the floor and Brandt wanted to finish him so badly that it took all his control not to strike the final blow and kill him. Brandt had a use for him and he would keep the man alive to carry that out. Kicking Arni's sword away and taking his daggers, Brandt backed away from the bleeding man on the floor. As he drew in deep breaths, exhausted from this fight, Kolga screamed and would have charged him if Thorfinn had not reached her first, taking her wrists in his hand and holding her away.

'You will not get away with this, Thorfinn. You stood behind me in this. You agreed to marry me to carry out this plan.'

'I did not,' Thorfinn yelled, shaking her as he did so. Then he lowered his voice. 'I married you...' Brandt waited for the explanation.

'Because she carried your child?' Katla asked.

Katla? By the gods, what was she doing here?

'You should be far away from here, Katla.' He said it even as he rejoiced in seeing her. She walked towards him, but stopped before Thorfinn...and Kolga.

'She told you she was pregnant and you so wanted the son she promised that you married her.'

'Aye.' The word came out as a sad, defeated whisper.

'And then she turned you against me, telling you I was not yours.'

'Aye.' The terrible sorrow spoke of such a loss in that admission.

'She is not yours and you still protected her,' Kolga said, pulling herself free of Thorfinn's grasp. 'And she caused me to lose our son! I asked her for help and she killed our child!'

Brandt was shocked, yet Katla did not seem surprised by this at all. He walked to her and reached out to her when Arni spoke.

'You told me it was my child. You told me you lost our child,' Arni accused.

Brandt could not feel sorry for the man. Liars all of them, but he'd been played a fool by this woman. As had Thorfinn, from the sound of it.

'She sent her maid to me for a potion. I only gave it to her because she was desperate. But I witnessed her turning it over to Kolga that day.' She held out her hand to Brandt. 'Until you said something last night, I had forgotten all about it.'

'You lying bitch!' Kolga called out, running at Katla with one of Arni's daggers that she'd grabbed off the floor. Brandt turned to try to protect her, when suddenly Kolga stopped and blood poured from her mouth.

Thorfinn's sword pierced her from behind. He twisted it once before using his foot to push her off it. She was dead before her body landed on the floor. Thorfinn yet held the sword out and Brandt gathered Katla behind him. He did not believe the man would harm her, but his senses were reeling from the surprise revelations he'd just heard. Instead, Thorfinn turned the blade and held out the hilt to Brandt.

'I believed her. I believed her against my daughter, against my friend, against my King,' he confessed. 'She convinced me that Katla was the product of your father's betrayal with my wife which I know now is not true. She made certain to divide us and pit us against each other. All the lies. All the lives lost.' He fell to his knees and bowed his head to Brandt, offering his life in return for his sins.

He heard Katla's indrawn breath behind him at Thorfinn's words. The man had raised her as his own for most of her life until his weakness had led him to reject her. What should he do? The man should die for his part in the plan to destroy Brandt's family. And yet, Thorfinn had saved his life and even allowed his escape, never expecting him to return.

'You will come with me to the King and stand witness to her guilt.' He nodded at Kolga's body. 'Arni will be judged for his part in this. After my father's honour is restored and my lands and title returned to me, I will decide on your ultimate punishment.' Thorfinn nodded and then called guards and servants to take away Kolga's body and to move Arni to the cell below.

Katla stood silently watching and waiting until the hall had been cleared. Brandt waved off Thorfinn, for he had no wish to speak with the man at this moment. Alpia rushed from the hall to find Gemma, who had accompanied Katla back.

'I am guessing that you do not understand the part of marriage that requires a wife to be obedient to her husband? I gave you instructions to go south.'

'Aye, you did. But since I had sent you back to do my bidding—'

'Kill him, you said.'

'My bidding...' she nodded and leaned in nearer to him '... I felt that I should come and help you after all.'

He pulled her into his arms and held her. He could have lost her this day. He could have died and she

would have been at the mercy of his aunt and her ac-
complice who had none. A shudder raced through him
at the thought of her vulnerability because she had
followed him back. Brandt wanted to tease her then,
but the terror of what could have happened to her tore
him apart.

'Promise you'll try to obey me, Katla. I cannot risk
losing you.' He kissed her and she sighed against his
mouth.

'You will not lose me, Brandt. Worry not, I will be
at your side.'

She kissed him then, stroking down his arm and
holding him close, soothing his fears. It was insulting,
but after what they'd just experienced he allowed her
to do it. What he truly wanted was to take her upstairs,
find a chamber with a comfortable bed in it and keep
her with him until he was certain she carried his child.
When he lifted her in his arms and turned, his way was
blocked by Alpia…and Gemma. With her chin jutting
out and her narrowed gaze, the girl looked none too
happy about something.

'She would only come along quietly if I made her a
promise,' Katla explained as Brandt, with some reluc-
tance, set her on her feet.

'And what did you need to promise her?'

'Gemma, tell Brandt what you asked for?'

Something told Brandt he was going to laugh, in
spite of his efforts not to do so. From Gemma's glare,
it was clear she thought this promise a serious one.
From the smile that turned the corners of Katla's mouth
into the beginnings of a smile, he knew it was less so.

'Katla told me that if I came along and things worked out...' Gemma began. She waved her hand out across the now empty hall with the injured and dead bodies removed. 'As they have, she told me I could come and live with you in Maerr.'

'If that is your wish, you may,' he said. The request was not a hard one to fulfil and Brandt nodded. 'Katla?' He held out his hand to her, still hoping to find that bed.

'That is not all, Brandt Sigurdsson.'

'What else do you require, then?' Katla had taken his hand and now squeezed it in warning.

'I wish you to find me a Norseman like you for my husband. Not too old. Not too stupid. And not too arrogant.'

Brandt did not even bother to try to hold it in. He leaned his head back and laughed aloud, letting out the sorrow and drawing in the hope that Katla had given him. Then he nodded at Gemma.

'I think I may have a few possibilities in mind, Gemma.'

Gemma nodded and Alpia walked away with her, whispering to her as they left.

'That is high praise from her, you know?' Katla said.

'Not too old, stupid or arrogant?'

'She has high standards.'

'I am only glad that you did not. That you gave me a chance, Katla. I will be in your debt for ever for your help in proving my father innocent of treachery. My family is in your debt.'

He leaned down and picked her up in his arms,

wrapping her up tightly in his embrace and kissing her. Then, before anyone interrupted him again, he carried her to her bedchamber and they were not seen for days.

Epilogue

The fullness of spring lay on the lands in the kingdom his father had claimed before him and that he claimed in his name. The sun rode high in the skies and the nights were shorter and shorter. The crops grew in these longer days and promised a plentiful harvest for their efforts. Though it yet felt strange to walk among the lanes and paths of the village, it also felt good.

Good to be home after so many years of hiding and running.

Good to be home and have his brothers around him.

Good to be marrying a woman who loved him and who'd stood by him in his worst hours.

His father's innocence had been proven to King Harald and his cousin Eithr removed from the throne, making Brandt the King of Maerr. All traces of Kolga's treachery and crimes had been wiped away and her lands and those that Thorfinn forfeited as part of his punishment had been joined with Brandt's to give his family even more power and wealth. All that was left for them was to make their marriage official with the celebration being held on the morrow.

He'd asked his brothers to gather with him this night, the night before his wedding, disregarding part of the traditional ceremony he should have performed alone or with only his father or a close older relative. Instead, he'd asked not only his brothers—all of them—to help him, but also he'd invited the women they each loved to join them.

With torches in hand, Brandt led the group out of the village to the barrow where their ancestors and kin had been buried and beyond it to a smaller clearing among the dense trees. When they'd buried Sigurd after the attack, they had decided to bury him outside the customary place. Things then had been in turmoil— Sandulf had fled on a ship to the east, Alarr was grievously wounded and it was feared he may not survive, and his other brothers were going into hiding. Those dark times had made it unsafe to bury Sigurd where his grave could be disturbed by enemies.

As they reached the grave, they encircled it. Looking from one to another and then another, Brandt saw the best parts of Sigurd in each of his father's sons— loyalty, courage, honour, strength. Then he took Katla's hand and kissed it. She had been his support and had made it possible for him to reclaim the honour of his family and he would love her for ever. Their marriage on the morrow would simply be a public expression of the vows they'd sworn to each other, but Brandt wanted to make this part of it.

When everyone was in place, they put the torches into the ground to light the area and Alarr handed out the shovels. He and his brothers began to dig slowly, until they reached the grave goods they'd buried with their father's ashes. There, wrapped in heavy canvas, was his sword—the one he'd raised in battle. The sword he'd raised to protect his family. The one he'd raised in loyal service to his King.

Rurik, who'd been at Brandt's side north of Maerr when the massacre happened, lifted it out of the ground and shook the dirt from the bundle. He held it out to his twin Danr who untied the leather strip around it and peeled open the layers of material covering the sword. Carrying it over to the edge of the gravesite, Rurik turned to Sandulf, their youngest brother, who took the sword and held it out before them, offering it to Brandt.

Brandt hesitated, instead looking from one brother to the next until he'd met the gaze of each. Reclaiming their father's lands and title had cost them much in time and suffering and yet, glancing now at Breanne and Ceanna and Sissa and Annis and his beloved Katla, he knew the price paid had been well worth it.

'Do you wish to take this sword?' Alarr, the last brother to complete this tradition, asked.

Brandt understood that this was more than claiming a buried sword for use in his wedding ceremony. Or even promising to keep this for his firstborn son. This was his commitment to his brothers to carry out their father's destiny—to be King of Maerr. For a moment, a wave of anxiousness passed through him as the memories of all that had brought him here now and the possibilities of all the tomorrows rose up in his thoughts.

'I have asked her to be gentle with you, Brandt,' Danr jested. 'Go on now and take it.' The laughter that followed his taunt broke the tension and Brandt nodded.

'I do wish to take this sword,' he said.

He reached out and Sandulf placed it in his hands. The soft touch of Katla's hand on his back made him smile then as he took the sword by the hilt and held it out before him.

'Father, you have been avenged,' he called out into the night. 'The sons of Sigurd have regained all that was lost.'

His words echoed across the clearing and, as he lowered the sword and pulled Katla closer, he noticed that others had followed them. His mother Hilda and her husband Joarr watched, as did Thorfinn and Alpia and Gemma and others who'd supported them in the battle to clear their father's name of treachery. As Brandt watched them draw closer, he realised that he and his brothers had gained so much more than they had lost.

Brandt lowered the blade and wrapped the material around it once more. He would clean and sharpen it before the ceremony and it would gleam in the light of the sun and bring the gods' favour on his marriage. He hoped and prayed that the sacrifices being offered this night, and on the morrow by the holy woman and priests, would please them. Turning to Katla, he touched his mouth to hers and smiled.

'So, will you be gentle with me on our wedding night, Katla?' he asked in a whisper only she could hear.

She lifted up on her toes and kissed him more fully, tasting his mouth with her tongue and sliding her arms around his shoulders to hold him close. His flesh rose between them and she pulled back from the kiss to laugh.

'Must we wait until after the wedding?' she asked in a tantalising whisper that teased him body and soul. He tucked the sword under his arm and kept her within the embrace of his other as they started back to the long-house, followed by the rest of his family and friends.

'I would like to practise that part of our marriage a bit more. I am not certain we've got it right yet,' he said. A lie, a bold lie, for that was something that was completely right between them. In spite of her fears. In spite of her past.

'I do think you need to practise more,' she said, loud enough for his brothers to hear. Damn, but she would pay for that.

'Danr could offer some advice,' Sissa offered, as she peeked around Danr to look over at them. 'He plays *tafl* well.' Brandt and his brothers knew full well that his brother was not playing a board game with his woman and what skills Danr was known for from his younger days.

'Rurik and I have been married for more than a year now. I'm certain he could make suggestions,' Annis offered.

'We know how to do it well,' Breanne, Alarr's wife, said, sliding her hand down over her growing belly. 'We could share our knowledge with you.'

Alarr grabbed his wife and kissed her, covering her hand with his. They exchanged glances that spoke of love and Brandt could see the protectiveness in his brother's gaze. When Alarr glanced over at him as he set Breanne on her feet, Brandt saw the acknowledgement from his brother who now worried over his wife. Katla and Brandt had that same news to share with the others, but had decided not to announce it until well after the wedding.

Katla's laughter at each offer of advice warmed his heart. For so long he'd been filled with bitter rage and grief. Somehow, the daughter of his enemy had broken through that and forced him to live and forced him to care once again.

For that, he would love her till the end of his days.

They reached the longhouse and, after everyone went their own way, Brandt made good on his promise to practise. His brothers thoughtfully found other places to sleep that night. Katla made good on hers to be gentle with him…until she was not.

Their wedding feast lasted for three days and nights and was filled with kith and kin and joy and celebration…and many jugs of mead sent north by the brewers of Wik Castle for their lady's pleasure. Brandt tried to warn everyone about the effects of the potent brew, but his words went unheeded and many heavy heads met the morning's bright light.

Though he wanted his brothers to stay for the summer, they could not. So, each brother left to go home— to Northumbria and to Strathclyde and to Skíð and to Éireann—with promises to return to celebrate the birth of Brandt's heir when that happened. No one knew that child would arrive sooner than they all suspected.

And with the coming births—Alarr and Breanne's, his and Katla's, and any others to come—the sons of Sigurd would begin welcoming the next generation into their family.

* * * * *

If you enjoyed this story, be sure to read the first four books in the Sons of Sigurd collection

Stolen by the Viking
by Michelle Willingham

Falling for Her Viking Captive
by Harper St. George

Conveniently Wed to the Viking
by Michelle Styles

Redeeming Her Viking Warrior
by Jenni Fletcher

Author Note

In September 2018 I received an email from an author friend asking if I'd be interested in joining a multi-author Harlequin Mills & Boon Historical Romance project set in the Viking era. Though I usually focus on Highlanders, the invitation and the project grabbed my interest. And the other authors involved—Michelle Willingham, Harper St George, Michelle Styles and Jenni Fletcher—were some of my personal favourites. So I said yes.

Two years later my story, *Tempted by Her Viking Enemy*, completes the five-book series and finishes the quest of the **Sons of Sigurd** to discover and bring to justice those responsible for their family's destruction.

Email discussions, spreadsheets, Word docs, a Facebook authors' group, phone calls and consultations with editors followed as we plotted and planned the series over the next months. We needed to decide timing and settings and locations and *so* many family details! It was fun and confusing and a challenge to collaborate with the other four while each of us was sorting through our own plots and characters. But, wow, the results were worth all the effort.

When I was asked to write the final book I was honoured—and terrified! After working with the others to set everything up, I would need to pull all those threads together—clues, romances, family details, plot twists, history and fiction—and tell the final story of the Sons of Sigurd.

Oh, and have a good story that focused on the romantic relationship of the eldest son and the daughter of their enemy! No worries!

After more than a year of combined writing time among the five of us, the series is now complete and I love the way it has all turned out! Five sexy, brawny Viking warriors and the strong, brave women who fall in love with them. Stories set in places from Viking Norway and Ireland to Pictish Scotland and Saxon England. Intrigue and a mystery with clues to follow.

All five Sons of Sigurd are waiting for you now and I hope you, dear reader, will give each of them a try.